Pawns

THE LYONS GARDEN BOOK THREE

D.M. FOLEY

REMEMBER YOUR ROOTS PRESS

ISBN-13: 979-8-9891130-2-6 paperback

ISBN-13: 979-8-9891130-3-3 Hardcover

ISBN-13: 979-8-9891130-4-0 Ebook

Cover Design by: Dawns Designs

Printed in the United States of America

This book is dedicated to every one of my readers who leave reviews, make recommendations, send me letters, and send me messages through social media with words of encouragement. You all keep me motivated to write more.

Thank You!

Contents

"In life, as in chess, one's own pawns block one's way. A man's very wealth, ease, leisure, children, books, which should help him win, more often check-mate him." Charles Buxton

CHAPTER ONE

Surprises

J ESSICA'S HEART HURT. HER chest was still tight. She found it hard to catch her breath. The tightness, caused by losing her sister, her best friend, left a gaping hole in her universe, which was unbearable. She only just functioned after the death of her youngest brother, days after her sister's death.

Each week, the calls from Anne, her agent, went unanswered by Jessica. This had Timothy, her fiancé, worried. His editor called with jobs for both of them as well. He declined each time. Jessica was in no shape to work. He could not fathom leaving her in this mental state.

The tightness in her chest had gotten worse.

"I think you should get checked in the emergency room, just to make sure nothing more serious is going on with you."

"It's just grief, Timothy. No one has died of a broken heart."

"I am not so sure of that. Do you want to be the first one? That isn't what I want. We are going to the hospital to get you checked out."

"Okay. But, I am telling you, it will be a waste of time."

The drive to the hospital was short. In the emergency room, when Jessica filled out the form stating she had chest tightness and some breathing issues, they brought her into triage right away. Jessica tried to understate what she was experiencing while the nurse took her blood pressure and other vital signs.

"There is nothing wrong. My fiancé wants me to get checked out. I think it's just grief and stress. Within days of each other, I lost two of my siblings."

"I am sorry for your loss. It could be just the stress of your losses. However, your fiancé is correct in getting you checked out. I am sure he doesn't want to lose you."

The kind nurse made a valid point, and Jessica looked at Timothy. His green eyes watched the nurse with scrutiny and paid close attention to the numbers she was writing. His brow furrowed, and he rubbed his cheek with his hand. She could tell he didn't understand the numbers, which added to his concern.

She reached for his hand, took it, and squeezed it. It was her attempt at reassuring him she would be okay. The nurse showed them to a cubicle with a hospital bed, and another nurse hooked up the leads to an EKG machine to check her heart.

The doctor came in to examine Jessica. After discussing her symptoms and the concerns Timothy had, he ordered a full workup of blood work to rule out anything serious.

The emergency room had a steady flow of patients. The nurses and doctors were working hard to take care of them all. Jessica felt guilty because she didn't feel she needed to be there. Timothy sat with patience by her bedside, praying nothing serious was wrong with her.

The doctor returned to the cubicle two hours later to discuss the test results.

"Ms. Greenhall, your heart is in great shape. You are not at risk of a heart attack. However, you are anemic. Could you be pregnant? Anemia is fairly common in pregnancy. You stated you had your last period eight weeks ago."

"Irregular periods are normal for me. I never considered being pregnant. However, now that you mention it. I've had a queasy stomach. I just attributed it to stress and emotions."

"We can run tests for pregnancy. We will go from there."

Timothy stared at Jessica. The possibility of the woman he loved carrying his child brought up a bunch of emotions. His heart fluttered, and his palms were sweating. He thought of being a dad. He grinned, trying to hide his terror.

Jessica returned from using the bathroom and provided the urine sample to be tested. The nurse drew more blood. She wasn't sure how to feel. Her dream was to be a mom. However, she feared the timing wasn't right. They still didn't know who was trying to kill the family. The thought of their child becoming a target swirled in her mind. She prayed the tests would come back negative.

While waiting for the results, Jessica voiced some of her concerns to Timothy.

"What will we do if I'm pregnant?"

"What do you mean what will we do? We are going to love this child with all our hearts. We want a family and we will make it all work."

"What about the issues on the island?"

"What about them? I won't let anything happen to you or our child, Jessica."

The doctor interrupted their conversation when he returned to the cubicle.

"Ms. Greenhall, the tests revealed you are indeed pregnant. Therefore, I will prescribe you some iron pills and prenatal vitamins. Also, I recommend you get in touch with your ObGyn Doctor as soon as possible."

Jessica's heart sank. Timothy squeezed her hand and looked into her eyes. What she saw was determination. His resolve erased her trepidation.

"Oh, thank you, Doc. I will."

A nurse came in and gave Jessica her discharge papers. As they left the emergency room, Jessica felt a range of emotions. The tightness in her chest eased up. A warmth radiated from her heart as if the pieces were mending together again. Hours earlier, hopelessness filled her, and she struggled to hold on to the will to live. Now, she would do everything to keep this child growing inside her safe. Keeping the secret would be vital until they felt the threats against them were gone.

"Are you okay, Jess? You are extra quiet."

"Yes, I am fine. We can't tell anyone about this. No one. And we must move up the wedding date. Perhaps move the wedding off the island altogether."

"Whatever you want, dear. I want to keep you happy and safe. Both of you."

Timothy was beaming at Jessica, stealing glances at her while driving them home.

"It's just I want to keep our child safe. I still feel like there is a black cloud following us around. And I am scared."

"I understand. We will call Jimmy and tell him we changed the wedding date because of everything. I still think we can have it on the island. If we change that, I think we will raise more suspicions."

"Okay, but how will we keep ourselves safe on the island? Every time we go there, someone dies. I feel like I am the bringer of death."

"Jess, honey, you are not the reason they died. Samantha and David would never want you to feel guilt for their deaths. If we have a girl, we can name her Samantha, and if it's a boy, we can name him David."

The tears trickled down Jessica's cheeks. Timothy always had the answers. The idea of naming their child after either her sister or her brother helped to soothe her broken heart. Whether their baby was a boy or girl, they cherished and loved them already.

They had ordered some food from Village Pizza and picked it up on their way home. Jessica realized hunger ravaged her. The barbeque chicken pizza hit the spot. After dinner, they set about calling Jimmy to let him know they needed to move the wedding date to April second. That would give them four weeks to throw the wedding together. Jessica prayed that their caterer, photographer, and DJ would all be available for the new date.

Jessica dialed Jimmy's number. Her heart raced, and her brows furrowed when it took a couple of rings for him to answer. Usually, he was quick to pick up the phone. She breathed a sigh of relief when he answered.

"Hey Jimmy, how are you doing?"

"Oh hey Jessica, I guess I am doing as well as expected. And how are you doing?"

"Honestly, I am struggling. I'm trying to get back to normal, but it's hard processing everything that happened."

"Understandable. You have suffered a terrible loss."

"About all that. Any leads?"

Jimmy took a deep breath and released it. He wished he could tell his cousin they had something to point them toward who had been terrorizing the family. He sought evidence that her sister and brother's deaths were not accidents, as they suspected. But he couldn't find any.

"None. Rich and I have been working nonstop to figure it all out. I think he is working harder than I am. To keep his mind off the loss of your siblings. Not to mention the breakup."

"I appreciate everything you two are doing. Since you mentioned the breakup. I am thinking of asking Danielle to take Samantha's place as my maid of honor. But I know I need to talk to Rich first."

"I'm not sure he will be okay with that. Keep in mind also that Danielle might not even set foot on the island again."

"I will talk to him and to her. On another note. Concerning the wedding. Tim and I have changed the date to April second. I hope that is okay. I know it is short notice and all. We want to bring some happiness to the family after all that has happened."

"Of course, Jessica, whatever you two want is okay with me. I might hire outside security, though, for that day. To be extra safe. We are still understaffed with the loss of Zach and Matt from the security team."

"I appreciate that, Jimmy. I knew you would understand."

"Of course. Hey, your brother just walked in. You want to talk to him now?"

"I might as well, thanks."

Jimmy handed the phone to Richard Jr.

"Hey Rich, how are you holding up?"

"Eh, I am hanging in there, and you?"

"I am coming out of my fog. However, I need to make some decisions regarding the wedding."

"What does that mean for me? Unless you guys have eloped."

"No eloping here. With Samantha gone, I have no maid of honor."

Richard Jr. winced at the mention of his kid sister's name.

"What do you want me to do? Be your maid of honor and be Timothy's best man? Wear half of a dress and half of a tux?"

"Hilarious. No, I don't have a lot of close girl-friends. But Samantha and Danielle are the closest best friends I have ever had."

Closing his eyes at the mention of Danielle's name. He felt the ache in his heart. The realization hit him that his sister was asking his permission to ask his ex-fiancée to be her maid of honor. He didn't want to hurt his sister any more than she was already hurting. The need to swallow his pride and deal with the pain of losing Danielle to appease his sister was overwhelming.

"Jess, if you need to, ask Danielle, and if she accepts. I will have no problem. Of course, seeing her will hurt. I love her and always will."

"Thank you, Rich. I love you."

"Love you too, Sis."

Jessica hated hurting her brother more than he was already hurting. She hoped that maybe there was some redemption in his and Danielle's relationship. The hope of getting them back together at the wedding was there. Her next phone call was to Danielle.

"Hey Danielle, how are you doing?"

"I am okay, Jess. How are you? I can't imagine what you're going through."

"Thanks. I am doing okay. I am calling to ask you something."

"Jess, I can't go back to Richard Jr. right now. If that is what you are thinking."

"No, of course not. I can understand your concerns, but you know Rich still loves you."

"I'm aware. The love I feel for him is still there, too. That's why I let him go."

"Would you be able to handle seeing him for just one day? For me?"

"I don't know… it's hard. He was my best friend."

"I understand. Samantha was my best friend, and losing her has been the worst thing I have ever dealt with."

"I am so sorry."

"It's okay. You are my next closest girlfriend, Danielle. That's why I want you to be my maid of honor."

"Oh my, Jess. It would be my honor. Yes, I will suck up my feelings for one day. As I am sure, he will too."

"Thank you. Oh, we moved the date to April second, though."

"Okay. Tell me what to do."

Jessica felt a renewed sense of excitement about the wedding as she talked to Danielle about what she needed help with. When they hung up, she had begun to feel some hope that the wedding would be perfect. But she just had one more phone call to make. She needed to have some legal documents done.

Arthur was more than happy to help her and Timothy. Divulging their secret to him, he swore to secrecy. It was an attorney-client privilege, anyway. Together, they made sure their future child would be secure if something happened to them.

CHAPTER TWO

Truths

JIMMY GOT OFF THE phone with Jessica and stared at the envelope he had been holding. The name on the return address shocked him. Melissa Zimmerman. Just seeing her name on the envelope made his heart beat faster. He never expected to hear from her again after Zach's funeral.

He slid his finger under the flap and opened it up. It was a letter written on pink stationery with her flowing cursive handwriting. The faint smell of her perfume lingered on the paper. His eyes closed and his mind wandered to their younger years. The sweet memories of holding her hand and walking her home after school every day. He unfolded the letter and braced himself for what the letter might contain.

Dear Jimmy,

I hope this letter finds you well. My thoughts have revolved around what you said the last time we saw each other. Something you said made little sense to me. You said your parents are not your only family on the island. This has me thinking. Are you alluding that you are a relation to the Gardiners?

That is the only way your comment makes sense. It would explain why you were living in the Manor house as well. It is hard for me to figure out where your connection to them is. I know the Driscolls adopted you, as does everyone on the island, so I know there is a possibility that your biological parents somehow are part of the Gardiner family. I just don't know exactly who or how.

I know none of this is my business. However, it will help me understand why you won't choose me over the island. I believe you still love me as much as I love you. I see it in the way you look at me and I felt it in the bar when you kissed me. If you don't, and I am reading you all wrong, then I will understand if you do not answer this letter.

Your Friend Always,

Melissa

Jimmy was shell-shocked. Right there in black and white, Melissa had admitted she still loved him. She wanted him to choose her. He hadn't chosen her. Guilt rose in his chest. The desire to choose her was there. It had always been there. He felt so anchored to the island he grew up on, though, and he didn't know why. Up in his room, he found some stationery and started writing a response to Melissa.

Dear Melissa,

With everything that has occurred in the last several months here on the island, I am as well as I can be. I guess I should never have mentioned that in our last encounter, but since I did, I suppose I owe you some sort of explanation.

Yes, I am a Gardiner. My mother was Mary Gardiner. My father was Benjamin Timmons. They were having an affair behind Richard's back. Unknown to both of them, Benjamin was Richard's half-brother. The doctor revealed this information to Alexandria when she forced Mary to have a paternity test through amniocentesis. She had caught Mary and Benjamin in the act one day. It was through that testing that Alexandria found out who Benjamin was, although she did not share that information with them. When she found out Richard was not my father, she forced them to agree to put me up for adoption. They all conspired to tell Richard I died at birth. On Alexandria's deathbed, she revealed these secrets to me and my cousin Jessica. After we had agreed to DNA testing, to verify we were both Gardiner heirs.

While I am spilling my guts, I must confess. I do not believe your brother's death was an overdose. I believe his death was not accidental. A psychopath is targeting the Gardiner family.

I know your brother spoke to you about the deer carcass. He did so, per my request. There have been four. After each one except the last one, we found the hearts in the rooms of my cousins.

We believe we are all in danger, or at least those that are known Gardiners. I don't seem to be a target, since it is not public knowledge that I am a Gardiner. There is more. Jessica and Timothy intercepted Christmas presents that were addressed to each family member, except me. They were dead crows. We have researched the symbolism and have taken them as death threats. I will not sleep until I bring justice to this crazy killer. It is unfortunate we feel Zach was collateral damage because of his relationship with Samantha.

Love Always and Forever,

Jimmy

The letter sat in front of him. He folded it and put it in an envelope. Jimmy tucked it into the inside of his jacket. Since it was his day off, he could go to the mainland and put it into the mail. Melissa deserved some answers. He didn't know if it would help her or hurt her.

"Where are you headed to, my son?"

Stella was working in the kitchen as Jimmy walked through and headed towards the door.

"I have some errands to run. I will be home in time for dinner if Rich asks where I am."

Jimmy and Richard Jr. had become closer through all the craziness and he had called him Rich to distinguish his cousin from his uncle. They had become more adamant about sharing information as well. It helped them both to feel less anxious about the serial killer stalking the family.

"Okay, Jimmy. I will let him know. Be safe. I love you."

"I love you too, Ma."

Stella was very aware of the danger her son was in. She wished she could protect him. There was no way she could, though.

Jimmy took the ferry to the mainland. When he dropped the letter off at the post office, his heart raced. There was no taking back the information he shared. He hoped the information was enough to placate Melissa's curiosity. As much as he loved her, he prayed she stayed away. He could not stand the thought of anything happening to her.

While on the mainland, he stopped at the police station. He had asked for copies of all the police reports pertaining to the Gardiner family tragedies. The hope was that he could find some-thing, anything, to lead him to clues about who was tormenting the family.

"Hey Jimmy, here are those reports you want-ed."

Sergeant Rollins handed Jimmy the reports. They were friends from their high school days. Jimmy appreciated the professional courtesy he was being afforded.

"Thanks, Rolly. I appreciate the help. If I come across anything, I will let you know."

"You are welcome, Jimmy. I want answers too. If there is a serial killer in the area, that affects everyone."

"Rolly, as I explained before, I don't think this killer has aspirations to kill anyone other than the Gardiners. But if I have any inclination that things have changed, I will let you know."

Jimmy had some time before he was due back for dinner. He headed to his office and started go-ing through the reports. When Richard Jr. came into the security shack from patrolling, he just shook his head.

"Man, you are such a workaholic."

"I know I am. I can't rest right now, though. The bodies are piling up. And now with Jessica and Timothy pushing up their wedding date. I am eager to keep them safe."

"Yeah, I understand the anxiety. Did she tell you who she replaced as maid of honor?"

"Yeah, bud. I am sorry. That's gotta be rough."

"I will be fine. I just hope we can keep everyone safe."

"Yeah, me too."

Jimmy went back to poring through the reports. He smiled when he realized his buddy had also added the coroner's reports. Good old Rolly. Even though they came from different backgrounds, he had been the one true mainlander friend he had made back in high school.

Alexandria's accident/ homicide report was first. As he read through it, nothing new jumped out at him. He read through the pages of statements from those who had been in the house. Arthur, Stella, Martin, Betty, Mary, Jessica, and Timothy. Everyone seemed to have a reliable alibi, except Mary. Therefore, when Mary committed suicide and left a note stating she had pushed Alexandria, they closed the case. He reread Alexandria's statement made from her hospital bed.

It stated, "Victim states the perpetrator pushed her down the stairs. When asked by whom she mumbled something, got the sound b, out, and then went unconscious again. I assume she was attempting to say by. When asked the next time she awoke, she could not remember."

She knew. Alexandria had known who had pushed her. The injuries to her brain must have affected her memory. This knowledge only frustrated Jimmy even more.

As he read the statements, he pictured in his mind where everyone in the house was at the time of the incident. Stella had been in the kitchen, still cleaning up after dinner. Martin was cleaning the dining room. Betty was upstairs making sure all the guests had what they needed and checking on Mary. She stated Mary had not responded to her knock on her bedroom door. Mary had gone to her room earlier in the evening. Betty had assumed she had passed out. According to her statement, Mary said she only recalled she had drunk wine in her room. Timothy had been in Jessica's room with her. Arthur was taking a shower in his room. *Maybe Mary had been the one to push Alexandria?*

There was a knock on his office door. It was Samuel.

"Hey, Jimmy. I was wondering if I could have a few days off. I want to go away for the weekend with my lady friend."

"Sure, Samuel. Have a good time."

"Thanks. We will."

Jimmy rubbed his temples with his fingers. The answers had to be right in front of him. He closed Alexandria's file and opened Mary's.

This was going to be difficult. The scene etched in his mind of his biological mother's death. Reading through everything, nothing seemed out of the ordinary. Open and shut case of suicide. The toxicology report confirmed lethal doses of Xanax and alcohol. The tears welled up in his eyes. It seemed as if Mary's suicide was legit. The only thing that still didn't fit was the fact she could not have tried drowning Jessica. So why would she confess to that? Is there someone she could have been covering for?

Who was Mary close to? Then it hit him. Samuel. The one beneficiary of her estate. The one who seemed to care for her in a more intimate way by leaving flowers at her grave. Jimmy put his jacket on and headed to the garage. He needed answers. It was time to be blunt.

Samuel was under the tractor tinkering when Jimmy walked into the garage.

"Hey Samuel, you got a moment?"

"Sure."

Samuel rolled out from under the tractor.

"Look, I need answers. I am not explaining why I need to know them. All I am going to say is they are security-related."

"Okay. What do you need to know?"

"What was the relationship between Mary Gardiner and you?"

Samuel winced at the question. He shoved his hands into the pockets of his pants. It had been a while since he thought about Mary and their relationship. That was a part of his past he was eager to forget.

"I am going to answer only because you are in charge of security, otherwise I would tell you it's none of your damn business. Ms. Mary hired me. We met in town one day. I was having a hard time finding a job because of my injuries from an accident. I told her I had grown up on Gardiners Island, however, I had moved away for a while. She asked me what my skill set was. I told her I was a mechanic. She hired me. We became friends. I wanted more than friendship. She couldn't see herself with a lowly mechanic. When she had too much to drink, however, she came to visit me. She shared my bed frequently."

"You were lovers."

The revelation shocked Jimmy. It made him reflect. Could Mary have been protecting Samuel? He knew he had to be careful with his next questions.

"I guess you could have called us that, yes. Not in public, though. Except for once, she had me escort her to her cousin's wedding."

"Did you ever go to her in the Manor house?"

"Yes, occasionally, when she would call me to come to her."

"How did you avoid anyone else seeing you go to her?"

"She showed me the passageways."

Samuel knew about the passageways, and so did Mary.

"Did Mary tell you why she had tried drowning Jessica?"

"No, she didn't tell me anything about Jessica. It shocked me she confessed to that. She had come out to the garage the day I showed Jessica and Timothy the osprey nests on the ATVs. I didn't see her touch any of the ATVs, though."

Jimmy believed him. There was no reason for him to lie. Everything Samuel had said was un-verifiable and Samuel knew it. It would have been easier for him to lie and say there was no relation-ship. Jimmy was back to square one.

CHAPTER THREE

Connecting Dots

MELISSA OPENED HER MAILBOX. The pile of bills was not new. No surprises, as she shuffled through them. Until she reached the letter. Her jaw dropped. It had been only a couple of days since she sent the letter to Jimmy and here there was already a response. Her hands shook. The urge to rip open the letter was great. However, she could wait until she entered the house.

She didn't want her father to see her open the letter and ask questions, so she went up to her bedroom. There were flutters of nerves in her belly. The bed gave her some stability as she sat and read the words he wrote. The words on the page swirled in her mind. Psychopath. Murderer. He was a Gardiner. Zach's death might not have been an accident. As she read those words, her blood boiled. Questions started flooding her mind. Did her father know this information? She needed answers. Now.

When she stormed into the living room and assessed her mother was still out with friends, she knew she could unleash on her father.

"What exactly do you know about Zach's death?"

Her father looked up at her, puzzled. The anger in her voice was accusatory. The small pang of guilt stabbed at her heart.

"What do you mean, Melissa? Zach and Samantha died of an overdose. Nothing less and nothing more. Why are you bringing up such a painful subject?"

"What about the deer carcasses, Dad? On the island. What else are you keeping from me? What about Jimmy?"

"Woah, how do you know there was more than one carcass? I am not keeping anything from you.

The deer deaths on the island have no connection to Zach and Samantha's death. Yes, there is a psychopath killing the deer and tormenting the family with their hearts. What are you getting at asking about Jimmy?"

Melissa realized her father didn't seem to know anything about what Jimmy had told her in the letter.

"You really don't know, do you? Jimmy is a Gardiner, Dad. He was Mary's child. She had an affair with Richard's half-brother. She put the child up for adoption and lied about his death. Jimmy seems to think Zach's death was no accident."

"Hold on a second. What?"

Matt shook his head and couldn't understand the information his daughter was sharing with him. His heart hurt. The realization of what she was saying, and the implications, was just too much for him. He got up out of his chair and went to the kitchen. The beer he cracked open and took a swig of, choked back the tears welling up in his throat.

Melissa's demeanor shifted. Her stance softened as she followed her father into the kitchen and grabbed a beer for herself.

"You really didn't know. I am sorry. He loves me, Daddy, but he can't leave the island because of the family obligation. They are all in danger, except for him for now. That is only because it isn't public knowledge he is a Gardiner."

Matt looked at his daughter. She was a beautiful soul and deserved to find the right guy. Years ago, he felt that guy had been Jimmy. Guilt flooded him. How could he have missed all those connections? He had worked security for so many years side by side with Jimmy's dad and then Jimmy. He was a good kid. Now, knowing details he hadn't known before, he could understand the added stress Jimmy seemed to be under.

The guilt of leaving weighed heavily on his heart and mind. As he looked at his daughter, though, he knew he couldn't go back. He would do what he could to help Jimmy and the Gardiner family find the truth. So he went into the den and picked up the phone.

Jimmy sat in his office, poring over the reports for the fiftieth time. Nothing jumped out at him to point him in any direction. Each report led to more questions than answers. He jumped when the phone on his desk rang. Looking at the caller id, his brows furrowed when he saw Matt Zimmerman. Did he want to have this conversation right at this moment? Reluctantly, he answered.

"Hey Matt, how is retirement treating you? I hope all is well with you and the family."

"We are all doing as best as we can, Jimmy. I need answers, though. Melissa thinks I am holding back information. She filled me in on what you wrote. A lot makes sense to me now. I even understand why you kept it all secretive."

"I am sorry, Matt. It must be hard knowing I kept information from you. The premise was to keep everyone safe, but I failed."

"You didn't fail. We failed. It's a team effort. Even though I am no longer employed there and part of the team, I will do what I can from here."

"I appreciate the help. Can I send you copies of the reports I received from Rolly? Or would that be too much to ask? I don't want to open the wounds any wider than they already are."

"Send them, Jimmy. I will deal with the wounds. If it helps prevent more deaths and helps us get justice, I will gladly suffer."

"Thank you. I will make copies and put them in the mail. Yes, you can share it with Melissa. She might give us some valuable insight. The more eyes, the better at this point. Timothy and Jessica have moved up their wedding, and it is still here on the island. I need to keep them safe."

"I will do what I can."

"Thank you, Matt. And I am sorry I didn't trust you earlier."

"It's all good, kid."

Matt hung up the phone and went to get another beer. Melissa was sitting at the table brooding over the letter Jimmy had sent. She was deep in thought, almost in a trance. Then she looked up at her father with a look of complete understanding, as if a light bulb had turned on in her head. She pushed away from the table, stood up, and left the room.

"It all makes sense now."

The words trailed behind her as she ran upstairs. Matt just shook his head. When Melissa got to her room, she grabbed a pen and stationery and wrote a letter back to Jimmy.

Dear Jimmy,

Thank you for your honest response to my last letter. We are committing to helping you figure this all out. In doing so. I need to be completely honest with you.

It all makes sense now. Everything. Leaving the island was not a choice I wanted to make. I had to. Someone knows. Someone knew all those years ago that you are a Gardiner.

They didn't want us to be together. They warned me many times in numerous ways to leave you be. To leave the island. I was young and scared.

I found notes written to me to leave the island. To leave you. Warning me you were evil. Warning me that if I stayed, the evil would overcome me. I found dead crows at my window all the time. I wish you would leave the island too. I fear for your safety. Please be careful. I love you.

Love Always and Forever,
Melissa

Jimmy had followed through with his promise. He copied every report and overnighted it to Matt. The first report Matt started with was Alexandria's. Nothing jumped out at him. He understood Jimmy's frustration. Knowing Alexandria seemed to have known her attacker at first, but then couldn't remember. When he got to Zach's and Samantha's report, he choked back the tears. Reading the details didn't help him forget his loss. The toxicology report killed him to read. The list of drugs found in their system, alcohol, fentanyl, heroin, and trace amounts of GBH. Nothing they didn't already know. He still couldn't believe his son willingly injected himself, or Samantha. Neither of them were the type to do drugs. However, Matt was not naïve to the fact addiction could hit anyone at any time.

When Jimmy received Melissa's second letter, he smiled. At least they were communicating. It brought a sense of peace to his broken heart. The realization of what she implied in the letter, though, left him speechless. This psychopath had started a long game years ago. Sabotaging his relationship with Melissa. That much forethought took patience. A psychopath with patience was scary. It showed that this person had waited in the wings for a long time to execute their plans. What caused them to speed them up, though? Then it hit him. If this person knew about him, why wasn't he being targeted? What was his role in this?

He had lived on the island his entire life. Oblivious to the fact he was a Gardiner by birth. No threats were directed towards him, ever. They still weren't. This still bothered him. And now, knowing they had threatened Melissa to stay clear of him all those years prior, he wondered why. The nagging in the back of his mind still drove him crazy. The beer cans had stopped, but he had stopped drinking completely as well.

In the meantime, Melissa read over the reports and the pictures Jimmy sent of the deer carcasses, hearts, and crows. The crows hit Melissa the hardest. She knew without a doubt the wheels of thought in this psychopath had been turning for quite a long time. Now they just needed to figure out who it was, and how to stop them.

CHAPTER FOUR

Weekend Plans

So, THE FAMILY THOUGHT they could outsmart them? Jessica and Timothy changing their wedding date didn't change their plans one bit. Everything would still happen the way they wanted it to. They already had plans for the weekend that would help eliminate some obstacles.

Their plans were being executed flawlessly, with no fingers pointing at them. This made them so happy. The thought of one day soon having everything they ever wanted. No, everything they deserved. Everything that was rightfully theirs would come to fruition.

They would eliminate everyone that stood in their way. Everyone. No matter who it was. The power inside them grew. As it grew, their attraction to holding even more power grew. Others must have been able to feel their power because they were already attracting potential lovers. They had been seeing one regularly.

The thought of sharing their newfound life with a potential love interest was exciting to them. But they couldn't divulge their secrets to anyone. The Gardiners would pay for every misdeed and every transgression they ever endured because of their secrets. They would have the last laugh and the last of everything. Literally.

As they packed for their weekend getaway, they felt a sense of pride. A feeling they admittedly had never felt before. They certainly never felt pride or praise from their mother.

The thought of their birth vessel, as they had become accustomed to thinking of their mother, brought back anger, disgust, and hatred. They remembered the day they had found their birth certificate among their mother's possessions. They were seventeen. The questions their mother re-fused to answer.

Yet, the truth revealing in her demeanor. The look of fear in her eyes. Disgust consumed her when they looked at them. The reminder of who they were and what she was on the island.

That was the day their mother died. It was the day they had hatched the plan. The one that would eventually give them what was theirs by birthright.

It amazed them that no one found similarities between their mother's death and Mary's death. Although their mother had committed suicide decades before Mary. And, of course, their mother was just a lowly inhabitant of the island. No one of importance, replaceable. In fact, they replaced her position within days of her passing.

That had been their first human kill. The first boost in energy. They had left the island for a peri-od afterward and came back. No one had missed them when they were gone. That was the blessing of obscurity.

The blessing of no one caring who they were or what they did. They had always blended into the crowd. Seen and unseen all at once. No prestige or position of power in life. Yet. It would come.

They would be sure to manifest their destiny and bring about the changes necessary for them to become who they were. With no regard for who they hurt in the process. No one had cared about them all these years. Why should they care about snuffing out the very essence of those who never cared?

Their lunch break was over, and their packing was complete. After their shift today, they would leave the island and take a trip to set in motion the next aspect of their grand plan.

CHAPTER FIVE

More Tragedy

GRIEF STILL ENGROSSED MIRA over losing Samantha and David. Her manicured nails had a chipped and rugged look to them. The curls in her red hair matted together to her head. Richard had to coax her to shower or bathe every other day. Eating had become almost nonexistent to her. Richard was content if he could get her to eat bites of toast and jelly along with sips of herbal tea. Her cheeks had become hollow and her eyes had as well. The sadness consumed her.

Richard's concern for Mira absorbed him and took over his grief. He mourned the loss of his children, but he was terrified of losing Mira. She had been his whole life and world for so long. He had given up everything for her and now he felt on the brink of losing her, too.

When their house phone rang, they were both surprised. Very few people had their home phone number, let alone called it. They had almost forgotten they still had it. Both had been ignoring texts and calls on their cell phones by well-meaning family and friends checking on them. It was Mira that answered the annoying ring of the phone.

"Hello?"

"Hi Mira, it's Lena. I have been trying to reach you every day on your cell. I know nothing I say or do will take away your pain. You are my oldest and best friend, though, and you and Richard should not have to go through all this alone. Steven and I are coming up for a visit this weekend."

"Lena, I appreciate the concern, but we aren't up for company."

"We aren't taking no for an answer. We won't stay at your house. But we are coming and we are going to throw you a small dinner party. Just the four of us. We will do all the work. Let us spoil and take care of you."

"Lena. We aren't up for it."

"Mira, you will never be up for it. Take small steps. Samantha and David would want you to keep living."

Mira closed her eyes at the mention of her children's names. Deep down, she knew her best friend was right. They would not want her wallowing in her self-pity and grief. They would want her to live her life to the fullest.

"Okay. Okay, you can visit. I am a mess. My house is a mess. I don't even know what food we have in the house."

"No worries. In the morning, we'll be over. We will pick up groceries. We will clean the house. You and Richard, clean yourselves up. Take care of yourself. Take a long soaking bath."

The tears streamed down Mira's face.

"Oh Lena, thank you for always knowing what to do or say. You are the best friend anyone could have. Thank you."

"No, thanks needed. That's what friends do. I love you. See you tomorrow!"

"Love you too."

As she hung up, Mira felt overwhelmed by the kind gesture from her oldest friend in the world. She followed her friend's suggestion and took a long soaking bath. Shampooing and conditioning her hair. It took a couple of comb-throughs to get all the tangles and mats out.

Richard was waiting downstairs with the Chinese takeout. Mira smiled. Her hunger had not returned. However, the gesture reminded her of the tender, caring nature of her husband. She couldn't refuse to eat. As the rice and vegetables hit her taste buds, she savored the flavors she hadn't had in some time. To her amazement, she finished the entire meal. There was a renewed sense of energy in her. Richard sensed the shift in mood and he relaxed his guard a bit. He smiled and took her hand in his.

Leading the way upstairs, he took her to their bedroom and loved her the way they had at the start of their relationship. It was the first tenderness they had shared in weeks. The moment brought peacefulness to them both. As they lay together in their bed, Mira shared the discussion with Lena through tears of grief, comfort, and peace.

They fell asleep in each other's arms, content for the first time since the tragic loss of their two youngest children.

True to Lena's form, she and Steven showed up bright and early the next morning. Mira gave Lena a long gripping hug, conveying her gratitude towards her lifelong friend. The four of them got to work cleaning the house, stocking the cabinets with food, and all the little things Mira and Richard had put off doing over the last few weeks.

At dinner time, the four friends sat and shared memories of their children growing up together. They laughed and cried while they ate the meal Lena had prepared for them all. When they finished, they all retired to the living room to finish drinking wine and visiting.

A knock at the door disturbed their conversation. Richard got up to answer the door. Much to his surprise, he found Samuel and Rita standing on the threshold of his doorway.

"Richard! Samuel and I are spending the weekend here in Boston and I couldn't be here and not swing by to see my daughter's best friend and the love of her life!"

Stunned by the surprise visit, Richard ushered them both in.

"Rita, Samuel, come in. How nice of you both to surprise us like this. Your daughter- and son-in-law are here visiting as well."

"I thought I recognized the car in the driveway! I knew it wasn't yours with the New York license plates."

As they joined the others in the living room, they exchanged hugs with all.

"Mother, what are you doing here?"

"Lena, I am visiting a dear friend, just as you are. Is that not allowed?"

They could cut the tension between mother and daughter with a knife. It was clear Lena did not approve of Rita's new beau.

"You can visit whomever you choose to. I am just surprised, that's all. You have been scarce with visiting anyone."

Mira felt the tension and wanted to help her friend.

"Rita, I am thrilled you and Samuel stopped by for a visit. The more the merrier, right Lena? Isn't that what you were trying to do, anyway? Let's go get more wine."

Steven, Richard, and Samuel started discussing fishing while Rita, Lena, and Mira went into the kitchen to gather more wine and wine glasses. When they returned, the men were in the middle of discussing a fishing trip.

"I hope this trip won't involve a boat?"

Mira couldn't help having flashbacks to the past and the sailboat accident Richard had survived.

"Oh, hell no! My feet will stay planted on shore, my dear."

"I concur. I am not a fan of boats myself."

Samuel shuddered as he stated his affirmation against a boating trip, too.

The friends finished several bottles of wine before the guests headed back to their respected hotel rooms. Richard and Mira were both feeling pretty drunk and hugged their friends, thanking them all for the great visit.

Mira stumbled up the stairs, fumbling with her clothes as she got ready for bed. Followed by Richard, who was also stumbling up the stairs. They both quickly passed out from the amount of alcohol they had consumed.

Smoke burned Richard's nostrils and woke him from his slumber. Frozen in his bed, he choked on the smoke filling the room. He tried to yell to wake up Mira. The terrifying truth was he could not speak or move. As the flames engulfed him and his lovely wife, he realized they were going to perish in the fire.

The heat of the flames woke Mira and she tried to move. Terror gripped her when she realized she could not speak or move. The blackness consumed her as she lost consciousness from the smoke and flames.

The sirens of the firetrucks wailed as they pulled up to the house. Flames, brightly flickering illuminating the pre-dawn sky, were engulfing the two-story home pushing out every window on arrival. Neighbors ran to the firefighters with terror-filled voices, telling them they believed the residents were still inside. When the rescue team assembled to go inside to search for the inhabitants, the command stopped them at the front door and told them it was too dangerous. The fire had grown too big to go inside without risking more lives. It became a surround and drown attack.

It took hours for the overhaul to become complete and for the remains of Mira and Richard to be found. When Lena and Steven pulled up to the scene, her heart was racing. A police officer stopped her from approaching too close. They watched in horror as officials carried two black body bags out of the house and put them in the coroner's van.

Lena felt faint, covering her face with her hands while dropping to her knees. Steven enfolded his wife in his arms as he tried to lift her and escort her to their car. Her best friend, they had been through so much together. The fear that Mira was gone forever gripped her with grief.

She had no siblings, and neither had Mira, so they were more like sisters. After getting Lena back to their car, Steven tried to get information from some officers on the scene. They couldn't confirm the identities of the two bodies found. The police would release the information when confirmation occurred and after the family notification was done.

The thought of Jessica and Richard Jr. learning of their parent's death snapped them back to reality. They needed to get home so they could be there for their friend's children. Too much tragedy had befallen the family already, and this was just another dreadful blow.

As they headed home, Lena knew she needed to call her mother. Rita was in Boston too, so she would certainly hear about the fire on the news. The cell phone rang several times before her mother picked up, and Lena rolled her eyes, thinking of what delayed her mother from answering.

"Hello, Lena. What may I owe this phone call from you for?"

"Mother, there has been a fire. A horrible fire! Mira and Richard might be dead. Their house is gone. They found two bodies. Identities not yet known."

Sobbing, Lena choked out the words. Not believing what she was saying could even be true, but knowing it was.

"Oh, my god! Please tell me this isn't true."

"I wish it wasn't, Mom. Steven and I are on our way home. The kids are going to need all of us to be there for them. "

"We will be on our way as well. Lena, I am so sorry. I know she was more than just a friend."

"Thank you, Mom."

It was a long trip home and Lena kept replaying the memories of her and Mira in her head. That first summer together, while she and Steven were off spending time with one another, Mira and Richard had started their secret affair. She recalled how she had found her friend clutching a breakup letter, and how she had rubbed her back and held her hair as she got sick. Neither of them realized at that moment Mira had been pregnant with Jessica.

As the memories poured through her mind, the tears freely streamed down her cheeks.

CHAPTER SIX

More Bad News

JIMMY SAT IN HIS office. Things had been quiet on the island. The roar of an engine and tires on gravel pulling up to the security shack interrupted the stillness of his thoughts. When he realized it was Samuel, his concern peaked. Samuel was supposed to be out of town until Monday, and he rarely stopped at the security shack.

When Samuel came into the shack and came directly to Jimmy's office, the hair on the back of Jimmy's neck stood up.

"Is Richard Jr. around?"

Samuel reached up to the back of his neck and nervously rubbed at it.

"No, he is out doing rounds right now. Do you need to speak to him? I can radio to him to come back to the shack."

"No. No, I need to talk to you. Alone."

Samuel closed the office door behind him and sat down. The creases on his forehead were deep. Adding to the anticipation and anxiety, Jimmy was feeling about what he needed to talk about.

"Is everything okay, Samuel?"

"Honestly, I don't know, boy. As you know, I went away with Rita for the weekend. We went to Boston. She insisted we stop and visit Mira and Richard. They are old friends of hers. Lena and Steven were there visiting. The visit went well. Until this morning. Lena and Steven went to stop by again, but the house had burned. Two bodies found, not identified yet."

"Oh, my god. Are you telling me Mira and Richard are dead?"

"They could be. Don't know who else the bodies could be. I figured I would come home to the island early and give you a head up. I am sure someone will notify you as soon as they identify the bodies."

"Thanks, Samuel. Sorry, your weekend got cut short."

"It's okay. I just am getting creeped out by all these tragedies."

"Me too, man. Me too."

Samuel left the office and the shack. Jimmy sat in stunned silence. He had been in Boston himself, following up on investigating Samantha's death. He had talked to several of her past co-workers. Asked if she ever did drugs or any kind of illegal substances. They had all said no. She had been a straight-laced hard worker. Which they all said was commendable since in the restaurant industry substance abuse is prevalent.

Jimmy had even driven past Mira and Richard's house and had seen they had company, so he hadn't stopped. The nagging in the back of his mind came back, but he shook his head and dismissed the thoughts.

It wasn't until Jimmy and Richard Jr. were sitting down to dinner that the knock at the door

Jimmy had been expecting disturbed them. Martin had led the state trooper into the dining room. Jimmy braced himself for the news and the reaction from Richard Jr.

"Good evening, sirs. Sorry to bother you at dinnertime and all. Unfortunately, I have some information to relay."

Jimmy and Rich both stood and motioned for the trooper to sit down. He stood, so they both stayed standing.

"We received word from the Massachusetts state police that there has been a fatal fire at your parent's residence, Richard. I am sorry. The coroner has confirmed this through dental records. Both your mother and father have perished. Your sister Jessica is being notified by the Connecticut state police as we speak. I am sorry for your loss."

Richard Jr. grabbed the back of his chair to steady himself. His thoughts raced as fast as his heart did. The pounding of his heart became deafening in his ears and his breathing quickened. His mom and dad were both dead. How could that be?

He looked at his plate of food sitting on the table and immediately wanted to hurl.

Jimmy shook the trooper's hand and showed him to the door. When he returned to the dining room, Richard Jr. had sat down at the table with his head in his hands, sobbing.

"I am sorry, cuz. What can I do?"

Richard Jr. looked at Jimmy.

"Let's catch the son of a bitch that is killing our family. You know, and I know this was no accident."

"I know. There is nothing tying any of the deaths together, though. No commonality. How the hell do we figure out who is doing this?"

"I have to call my sister. This is going to devastate her even more. Maybe she should call off the wedding? At least move it off the island."

"Call her. Don't let her move the wedding off the island, though. That will give whoever it is control. We need to take back dominance. We will protect them."

"Okay. But how?"

"I have some ideas."

Richard Jr. composed himself and called Jessica. When she answered the phone in uncontrolled gasps, he knew they had notified her.

"Hey Jessica, I am calling to see how you are doing?"

"Rich, I can't. This can't be happening. It's like a bad dream. No nightmare. How could I find my biological family and lose all but two members in six months?"

"I know. It doesn't seem possible. We need to figure out who is killing us off before it's too late."

"But, how? We can't even connect any of the deaths to each other. They made them all seem like accidents. And occurred in various places."

"Wait, that's it!"

Richard Jr. looked at Jimmy while he was on the phone with Jessica

"What's it, Rich?"

"The commonality. They all seem like accidents! Now to pinpoint who had access to all the crime scenes and the family."

"You might be on to something. We need to plan to lay Mom and Dad to rest, though, first. Then focus on investigating the so-called accidents."

They made plans for Jimmy and Richard Jr. to go to her house the next day to discuss funeral arrangements for their parents. Then Richard Jr. made the call to Arthur to tell him the devastating news.

"Hi Arthur, sorry to bother you this evening. I have some bad news."

"Hello, Richard. I hope it's not another death. I can't handle anymore."

"Unfortunately, that is exactly what it is. Mom and Dad's house burned with them inside it. They did not survive. I know this might bring up your own terrible memories of how your family passed away. I am sorry."

"Oh, Richard. I am so sorry for your loss. Your Dad was a good man, despite some of his past decisions. Your Mom was smart and gracious. Do you need help with anything?"

"Actually, yes. Can you meet us tomorrow at Jessica's house to go over arrangements?"

"Absolutely, I will be there."

Richard Jr. and Jimmy played pool and brainstormed ideas on how to figure out who was targeting the family. Jimmy was careful not to have a beer when Richard Jr. grabbed one for himself. He was also careful not to mention the thoughts running through his head.

He was the last person to see Samantha and Zach. Granted, he didn't know if they were dead or alive at that moment, but he couldn't shake the guilt of not going to the car. Then he was the last person to see David alive. He was the one that told David to go upstairs and fly his drone out the window. Now, knowing he was also in Boston at the time of the fire that killed Mira and Richard, he couldn't help thinking the psychosis was back, and he was the one targeting the family.

Jimmy decided he would call his therapist the next day. He needed to get all of his concerns off his chest. He would tell her everything and let the chips fall where they may. The cost of keeping his thoughts secret was too much. Losing more of his family was too high of a price.

Richard had several beers. When he finally felt numb, he stumbled upstairs to his room. As he lay in his bed, his mind wandered to Danielle. It was late, and he was drunk, but he didn't care. He needed to talk to her. So he dialed her number.

"Hello, Richard? It's so late. Why are you calling me?"

"My parents are dead. I love you, Danielle. I need you. Please come see me tonight."

"What? Are you drunk? How are your parents dead? What happened? I love you too, Richard, but I can't go there."

"There was a fire at their house. They didn't survive. Yes, I am drunk. Please come, I need you."

"Oh, Richard, I am so sorry. My heart is breaking for you, but I can't. You know that place is dangerous. Please tell me when the funeral will be, and I will be there, but I can not come to you. I am sorry."

"Please, I love you."

"I love you too, but I can't. You know that."

"Then I will come to you."

"You are drunk! You can't drive!"

"I need to see you."

"Okay, okay. I will be there shortly. This one time, only because I don't want you getting in a car and driving."

"Thank you, I love you."

"I love you too."

It was annoying how she let him manipulate her this way, but Danielle loved him and wanted to be with him. She had been missing her best friend. The way they had always shared every detail of their lives. From the mundane, routine, daily tasks to the more complex questions that arose in their brains. She knew he was hurting. He had lost so much in such a short amount of time.

Captain Bill was grumbling at the late-night passage across the bay on the ferry. Danielle was very apologetic. Thankfully, she still had a key to the Manor house and she let herself in and found herself in Richard's waiting arms.

He buried his head in her shoulder and released the tears he had been fighting to keep inside. She didn't realize how much she missed being in his arms until they wrapped around her waist, pulling her closer. Her hands reached up to his face, lifting it off her shoulder.

Danielle kissed the tears on his cheeks and then made her way to his lips. Oh, how she had missed his soft, warm lips. The heat rose in her cheeks and traveled through her body. Richard Jr. broke the embrace, picked her up, and carried her to his bed.

In the morning, she awoke to him kissing the nape of her neck as he cradled her. The feeling of contentment overshadowed her concern for her safety. She stayed longer than she had expected. When she finally rose to leave, he tried to coax her back to bed.

"I have to go, Richard. There is work that I have. I love you. I will call you later to make sure you are alright."

"Alright. I love you too. I have to get up anyway and head to Jessica's. We have a lot to go over. I will fill you in later"

CHAPTER SEVEN

Last Plans

GETTING OFF THE ISLAND was easier than they thought it would be. Others were gone too, which made it easier for them not to be missed. When they realized Jimmy would be in Boston also for the weekend, they laughed at how easily the kid made things for them.

Plans were falling into place, and no one suspected them. Their companion for the weekend was so oblivious to the purpose of the trip. Keeping them drunk kept them from suspecting anything nefarious.

Watching Richard and Mira's house was a bit frustrating when they realized that Lena and

Steven were there. They had to wait for the right time to execute their plans. It had been late when the guests stumbled out of the house.

The lights went out in the downstairs rooms, and the ones upstairs went on. When they went back off, they knew it was time to go into the house.

Assuming both occupants were just as drunk as their guests made things simpler. They found the key under the mat and chuckled that they had learned that through listening to the routine conversations in the Manor house.

They were careful not to make too much noise. Even though they knew the occupants were more than likely passed out cold, they didn't want to chance them waking up. That would make things messy. The gloves they wore to prevent leaving fingerprints as a precaution were cumbersome.

The stairs creaked slightly with each step they took in the darkness leading up to the master bedroom. Both occupants were where they suspected they would be. A smile crept over their face. Pulling the syringes out of the bag they brought with them. One for each of them. Neither flinched as they administered the paralyzing drug.

Next, they set the candles around the room. They needed to set the stage to make it look like a horrible accident. After they strategically placed the candles around the room and lit them, they threw the discarded clothes of the occupants on top of some of the lit candles, closed the bedroom door, and took the batteries out of the smoke detectors, replacing them with dead ones.

When they locked and shut the front door, they could already smell the clothes burning. They sat in the car with their companion passed out in the passenger seat, watching as the house became fully engulfed.

The neighbor must have woken up to the glow from the flames and alerted the fire department. As they drove away from the fire, the fire trucks screamed past them.

When they got back to the hotel they were staying at, they roused their companion just enough to get them back to the room. It annoyed them when they realized their companion was more awake than they had expected. The companion wanted to do more than just sleep.

The rush of adrenaline still pumping in their blood enhanced the experience. They noted this feeling. They would keep it in mind for after the next kill.

The next kill would be the grand finale. If all went as planned, they would get all the prestige they had always wanted. They would receive what birth rite entitled them to.

When they found out Jessica had moved the wedding date, it made them speed up their plans. They had four weeks to complete their grand scheme. Getting rid of Richard and Mira was the first step.

Three more deaths needed to happen, then it would be all theirs.

CHAPTER EIGHT

Realizations

JIMMY WOKE UP EARLY and called his therapist. Thankfully, she had time to talk to him. He got everything, every little piece of self-doubt and guilt out. What he told her was shocking. However, she assured him that everything he had said would remain confidential between them as patient/therapist protected. He felt better after talking to her.

When he was done, he met up with Richard Jr., and they headed to Jessica's house. Pulling up the driveway a few hours later, Jimmy's stomach churned. He hadn't been here since informing his cousin of her sister's death. Now here he was again visiting because of tragic circumstances.

Knocking on the door, a sense of déjà vu overcame him. Timothy opened it and the men entered the living room exchanging hugs, along with tears. Arthur joined them a short time after their arrival.

"I am so sorry for your losses."

Richard Jr. took the role of head of the family now, so he spoke first.

"Thank you, Arthur. We need your help. None of these deaths have been accidents. Proving it, though, is the hard part. There are no leads who could do this."

"How can I help?"

"We want to transfer ownership of the island and the business to you and Allison. Secretly. The only motive for wanting the family dead is what we own."

"Wouldn't that just put a target on my head, and Allison's, if something happened to you all?"

Arthur was nervous about this plan. He didn't understand Richard Jr.'s thought process.

"That's why I say secretly. If something happens to us, whoever is doing this will seize the opportunity to take control. Think about it. Dad hid in plain sight for years when everyone thought he was dead. Could someone else have survived that accident? If so, everyone on that boat was an heir to the estate. Even Benjamin, even though he supposedly didn't know."

Jimmy looked at Richard Jr., stunned. Why didn't he think of that? The thought of his biological father potentially surviving the boat accident oddly excited him and terrified him all at once.

"Wait, that makes sense! But who has access to the island, and us, that we wouldn't recognize as our relatives? I have seen pictures of David, David Jr., Samuel, and Dorothy. Your Dad knew them all very well, even Benjamin. How could any of them pass through our radar of recognition?"

It was Timothy who had a memory surface that he thought was insignificant at the time but now might mean something.

"Samuel was on the ferryboat with me the first time I came to Connecticut to visit you, Jessica.

The day I got a flat tire, and the threatening note appeared. He has scars on his hands and face and walks with a limp. Possibly injuries from the boat accident?"

Jessica shuddered, remembering that day.

"He was leading us the day I had the ATV accident, and he was less than sympathetic."

Jimmy recalled the conversations he had recently with Samuel.

"Samuel admitted to me he knew about the passageways and that he had an affair with Mary. He is about the right age to be Benjamin. But we still have no proof to link him to any of the deaths."

Arthur sat in complete shock. Could the theory be correct?

"Okay, let's get the legalities all in order. However, it will only transfer to us if all of you die. Which I hope does not happen soon. I still don't know how that will help catch whoever is killing the family."

Richard Jr. had it all thought out.

"After Jessica and Timothy's wedding, we will set a trap. We will fake our deaths. If our theory is correct, Samuel, or should I say, Benjamin, will come out of hiding to claim his fortune. Jimmy and I just need to keep us all alive until we fake our deaths. That will be the hard part."

They spent the rest of the day making the funeral arrangements for Richard and Mira. Their emotions ran up and down like a rollercoaster. They all felt hopeful the nightmare they had been living would soon be over. And then, the reality of the danger they faced would hit them like a punch to the gut.

It was late afternoon when Arthur, Richard Jr., and Jimmy left Jessica's house to head home. Jimmy was glad he wasn't driving because he couldn't focus on the road. All he could think about was the possibility of Samuel being Benjamin. His fingers tapped on the passenger side door, as he was deep in thought.

Richard Jr. could tell his cousin was brooding over something and broke the silence.

"Hey, what's got you all knotted up? You are tapping louder than a busted piston in an engine and your knees are bouncing like rubber bouncy balls."

"Dude, if Samuel is our guy, he is a master liar and deceiver. And he is my father. It's all a bit unsettling, to say the least."

"I understand. When my dad came clean with all of his deceptions, it threw me for a loop. I was so angry at him. But now, with everything that has happened, I understand. He just wanted to be with my Mom, have a family, and be safe and happy."

"But my father is the bad guy. I can't see a redeeming quality or reason for him killing everyone. His only reason is greed. If it were to keep everyone he loved safe from harm, self-defense would be one thing. It's not though. This is cold-blooded murder."

"We need to make sure we don't tip him off that we suspect him, though. So you need to rein in your feelings on all this. We can't let him get away with it."

"Thanks for the reminder. This is just a lot to take in. I will keep my cool in front of him. Thankfully, he is a sort of reclusive, so we have minimal interaction."

The men got home right around supper time. Jimmy entered the kitchen and sat down at the island counter. Stella was busy preparing dinner as she normally did. She stopped when she noticed Jimmy staring into nothingness with his brows furrowed.

"What's got you all stressed out, son?"

"I have a lot on my mind, Mom. All these deaths. They just make you thankful for every breath you breathe."

"Yes, a lot of loss and a lot of grief. Way too much for one family to handle. I am scared for your life. I don't want to lose you."

Jimmy got up and walked over to his mother. He wrapped her in a big bear hug and kissed her forehead.

"Don't worry, Mom, we got this and nothing is going to happen to me. I promise you that. I love you."

After dinner, Jimmy and Richard Jr. retired to the parlor to play some pool. Richard Jr. cracked open a beer and offered an unopened one to Jimmy. Jimmy frowned and refused.

"I can't. There is something you don't know about me, cuz. I should have told you before, but I was afraid and ashamed. I had issues seven years ago with alcohol and drug addiction. It got worse. I went to rehab and everything. With what is going on right now, I need to be really careful not to consume anything and get back into that cycle."

"Oh man, I wish you told me sooner. We are getting all the alcohol out of here. I don't want to be a reason for you to relapse. I got your back."

Jimmy let out a sigh of relief. It felt good to get that off his chest. True to his word, Richard Jr. poured out his beer and removed all the alcohol from the house.

Then both men went up to their rooms to go to bed. Richard Jr. called Danielle.

"Hello, Rich."

"Hi Danielle, I wanted to let you know when the funeral will be for my parents. It will be Thursday. Here on the island. Can you please let your parents know?"

"Thanks, Rich. I will let them know. I will be there."

"Thanks, Danielle. For everything."

"You are welcome. See you, Thursday Rich."

All Richard Jr. wanted at that moment was to catch the serial killer targeting his family. Then he could marry Danielle and live the rest of his life happy and content. Thinking of living happily and content, his mind wandered to his sister and his brother. They both would never get to live the rest of their lives. Thankfully, his parents had lived happily for many years.

His eyes welled up with tears. The ache in his chest hurt so much. He wished he hadn't removed the beer from the house. This was when he realized he had been using the alcohol himself to numb the pain of his emotions.

The realization brought a deeper understanding of what his cousin must have gone through with his battle with addiction. There must have been a deep pain that he had been trying to numb. Richard Jr. resolved to talk to Jimmy more about it in the morning.

Jimmy lay awake contemplating the theory of Samuel actually being Benjamin, his biological father. He wanted to confront him in the worst way. That would jeopardize everything, though. How was he going to keep his cool? The thirst for a beer grew.

He was so grateful that Richard Jr. had removed the alcohol from the house. It made it easier to resist the urge. The night dragged on and sleep eluded him. He wished Melissa were with him. Remembering the weekend and that she had met him up in Boston to do some digging on Samantha's past.

They had gone to dinner at the restaurant Samantha had worked in and questioned her co-workers. The co-workers had remembered Samantha fondly and had even remembered Zach, as he was a regular there until Samantha moved to the island. Even though they both paid for their own meals since it wasn't a date but instead information gathering, Jimmy had felt the undercurrent of feelings between them bubbling up to the surface more than once.

They shared a hotel room just out of convenience and cost. With each of them sleeping in their own double bed. That had been so hard for him. He had wanted to crawl into bed with her and hold her close, as he had as a lovesick teenager in the past, but he had restrained. That made him proud that he had learned self-restraint.

As he thought of Melissa and how much he loved her and wanted to end the killer's reign on the island so she could come back, he fell asleep. In his dreams, he faced off with his father, and his father confessed to killing everyone, including his mother. Then Jimmy took a pistol out of a drawer and shot his father.

Jimmy bolted awake, shaking with terror at what he had just dreamed. It was going to be a long day.

CHAPTER NINE

Going Back Again

J ESSICA WOKE UP EARLY in the morning. Sleep had become something of an enigma in her life. The last six months had brought more chaos than she could ever imagine. Finding her biological family, then losing most of them tragically to a series of tragic circumstances that a serial killer orchestrated.

Then, she was also adjusting to the knowledge of being pregnant and was trying hard to take care of herself. Which meant she needed to try to sleep and ease stress. The death of her biological parents made that difficult at the moment.

Her thoughts went to the discussion they had the previous day about who they thought might be killing off their family members. The revelation that it might be Samuel all along made her tremble. It all made sense, and the puzzle pieces seemed to fit perfectly.

Samuel had admitted to Jimmy he knew about the passageways in the Manor house. That gave him a way of almost drowning her without being caught. They knew it could not have been Mary because she was not wet, and Jimmy had investigated and found there was no way she could have done it, even though she confessed in her suicide note.

He was the one who showed Timothy and her which ATVs to take for their assignment and led the way along the trails. Did he purposely take them down that particular trail, knowing the throttle would stick? Also, knowing there were steep declines to the narrow edges of those trails.

He also could have easily used the passageways to gain access to Alexandria and push her down the stairs. Then using the passageways to escape without being noticed.

Timothy and Jessica had passed Samuel in the hallway on the way to their room on Christmas Eve. The night they found the gifts for the family members.

Jimmy and Richard had explained how Samuel had been out with Rita on valentine's night. The night Richard Jr. had proposed to Danielle. The same night, Samantha and Zach died.

He was the one who found David's body. And to top it all off, he had been in Boston when her parents died in the fire. He had access to every single crime scene.

He had a motive, if he was really Benjamin. The question was, did he kill Mary or did she actually commit suicide? Samuel had admitted that he had an affair with Mary in conversation with Jimmy. If he loved her, why would he kill her? Although she left him an inheritance. Did he know? Could that have motivated him to kill her? Samuel had also said how Mary only used him and didn't want an outward relationship with him because he was just a mechanic. Was that truth or a lie? Did Mary know Samuel was potentially Benjamin? Mary and Benjamin had been lovers prior to the boating accident. If Samuel was Benjamin and Mary was intimate with him, wouldn't she have known it was him? The fact that Mary confessed to things they knew she couldn't have done led them to believe she did not commit suicide.

Thinking about it all overwhelmed her. The rage she felt bubbling under the surface of her emotions from overlooking him in the past made her palms sweat and heart race. Then the sadness at the fact they hadn't told their parents of the dangers they faced added to the guilt she already felt for surviving while her brother and sister had died. All of this filled her heart with such pain. Then her heart raced faster with the possibility of catching Samuel and being able to raise her unborn child in peace and safety.

The tears welled up and spilled out of her eyes, down her cheeks, and onto her pillow. Timothy awoke to the sound of her crying. He rolled over and cradled her in his arms.

"What's the matter, my love?"

"This nightmare could be over soon. We might get our happily ever after. And Rich and Danielle might, too."

"That would be nice. Then why are you crying, though?"

"Guilt. Samantha, Zach, and David will never have their happily ever after."

"Ah, my dear, they wouldn't want you to feel guilty. Let's get up and eat breakfast. We need to make sure you and our little one stay healthy."

Jessica took a shower while Timothy went downstairs to make them both breakfast. The smell of bacon and eggs wafted up to their bedroom, and her stomach growled. That motivated her to get dressed a little more quickly.

When she made it downstairs, Timothy had her plate made and a glass of orange juice waiting for her.

"Ah, this all looks so delicious. Thank you!"

"Anything for you and our little one. Make sure you drink that OJ. It's filled with folic acid, and that's important for the baby."

Jessica chuckled. It didn't surprise her that Timothy had done research on pregnancy and the things she should eat and not eat. With him being a writer, research was his middle name.

"Yes, sir. Have I told you lately how lucky I feel to have you?"

"No, you haven't, but we can go upstairs after breakfast and you can show me your gratitude."

Timothy just smiled a flirtatious grin at Jessica and wiggled his eyebrows.

"Hmm, that's a possibility."

"Ooh, is that a promise?"

"Yes, if you promise to make this kind of delicious breakfast for the rest of my pregnancy."

"Deal."

Jessica and Timothy ate breakfast and then went upstairs, where Jessica fulfilled her promise to Timothy. Afterward, while Timothy showered, Jessica worked on their wedding plans.

She was revamping the seating chart. She wanted eyes on Samuel at all times. He would be Rita's plus one. Poor Rita. Jessica wondered how she was going to deal with the news that she was dating a serial killer.

Jimmy had already assured Jessica he was upping security for her wedding. He told her and Timothy that he was hiring his friend Rolly to be an undercover detective to follow Samuel the entire time. This made her feel they would all be safe during the wedding.

The catering was all set; the cake was all set, the photographer, the DJ, and even the bartender. She had hired Joe. Since David's funeral, she had kept in contact with him. She wanted to make sure he was okay. He appreciated her checking on him. David's death had more of an impact on him than he had expected, considering they hadn't known each other for long.

When Timothy came downstairs, he joined her in her office where she was working.

"Whatcha doing, my dear?"

"Rearranging the seating chart for the wedding. I want to see Samuel at all times. I know Jimmy is going to have a detective on him, too. The more eyes on him, the better. "

"Good idea. Did I ever tell you how incredibly smart you are?"

"Nope."

"Well, you are. That is just another one of the million reasons I love you so much. How about we go for a walk and take some pictures? It is a beautiful day and I feel spring is in the air."

"Sure, let me just finish this up."

When she finished Jessica grabbed her camera, and Timothy grabbed his notebook. He loved writing little snippets of descriptions of the things Jessica took photographs of. This had become a favorite pastime for them both. He loved watching her capture nature in her pictures. She conversely loved reading his descriptive words about the same things she was taking pictures of.

They had told his editor and her agent they were taking a sabbatical until after the wedding and their honeymoon. They planned on spending a month at their cottage in Ireland for their honeymoon. Jessica could not wait to get to Ireland. She felt safe there and relaxed. The relaxation and safety would be welcome after the craziness of the last few months.

When they returned home from their walk, Jessica packed for their trip to the island for her parent's funeral. She didn't want to go. The thought of saying a last goodbye to her biological parents filled her with an overwhelming sadness.

From the moment she found out about being adopted, she had wanted to know her birth parents. It took her years to find them. Now they were gone, along with her adoptive parents. At least she wasn't alone.

She had her brother Richard Jr. and her cousin Jimmy. Also, she had the love of her life with Timothy. What she would do right now, without him, she didn't know.

Timothy helped Jessica pack and then they headed on their way back to the island. He could not wait until they could stop going to that place. It creeped him out. The only good thing that had come from him going to the island in the first place was meeting Jessica. He had been a big fan of her photography. When Alexandria had mentioned to

Arthur that she wanted Jessica to do the pictures for Timothy's article, he was more than happy to request that his editor contact her agent. Now his focus was on keeping her and their unborn baby alive.

The trip to the island seemed to take such little time. The more they went, the quicker the route seemed to be. Captain Bill was solemn and offered his condolences as they boarded the rickety ferry to cross to the island. The new ferry would not be there in time for the wedding since they upped the date.

As they drove up to the Manor house, they passed Samuel working on the tractor. He always seemed to be working on that thing. He looked up from what he was doing and gave them a solemn nod as they went by. Jessica shuddered. She couldn't wait until they could prove he was behind everything and put him behind bars.

When they entered the kitchen, Stella stopped what she was doing and wrapped Jessica in a big hug. Jessica could not contain her tears and melted into Stella's motherly arms. Stella let Jessica stay in her arms until Jessica felt the need to break the connection.

"Thanks, Stella, I needed that."

"You are welcome, child. I am here anytime you need a hug."

Stella wiped the tears from Jessica's cheeks with her apron and then got back to fixing food for the funeral. Jessica and Timothy headed upstairs to their usual room. They bumped into Betty in the hallway.

"Ma'am, sorry for your losses. If you need anything, just let me know."

"Thank you, Betty. I appreciate the condolences and the hospitality."

By dinnertime, Jessica's grandparents had arrived. Her mother's parents were just fragments of the people they were before their two grandchildren and only daughter died. Jessica noticed the frailty. They looked as if they had aged twenty or more years in the last two months.

For the first time, she felt her grandparents were just like her. They seemed lost without their loved ones, too. Their eyes were red from crying and they hunched their bodies with fatigue and stress. It shocked them when she approached them both and gave them each a big, long hug. They weren't usually the affectionate type, however; they were receptive to Jessica's gesture.

Dinner was solemn. They discussed minor details about the funeral the next day. Jessica, Timothy, Jimmy, and Richard Jr. were careful not to discuss their theory about the deaths with the grandparents. When they were all done eating, they all retired early to bed. They knew all too well the next day would be emotionally draining on them all.

Jessica lay in Timothy's arms and tried to drift off to sleep. She was tired in every way possible, yet her eyes did not want to close. Then she was thirsty, so she went down to the kitchen. When she looked out the window, she saw Rita ascending the stairs to Samuel's apartment above the garage. She felt bad for Rita.

Rita had divorced her husband to be with Samuel. Unlike her cousin Mary, Rita wasn't ashamed to be seen with him. She found Samuel exciting, which kept her interested in every way. Jessica shook her head. She couldn't worry about Rita's feelings. The woman would get over it, she would have to. Their lives were more important than her feelings. When Jessica went back upstairs, she lay in bed with her hands on her belly and fell asleep thinking of her unborn child.

CHAPTER TEN

Goodbye Again

IT WAS IRONIC THAT Jessica got the best night's sleep she had had in a long time the night before her parent's funeral. Her body must have sensed she would need the strength to get through the day. The smells of breakfast made her open her eyes as her stomach growled. Timothy was already up and getting dressed.

"I didn't wake you, did I? You were sleeping so peacefully, I was trying to be extra careful not to wake you up."

"No, I think my hunger is what woke me up. The little one wants breakfast."

She rubbed her belly.

"Okay. do you want me to go downstairs and get a plate from Stella and bring it up to you? Or do you want to eat downstairs in the dining room?"

"I will get up and go downstairs. We have to start this day at some point."

As they descended the staircase, a bustle of activity was occurring at the bottom. People were preparing for the funeral. The bodies of her parents were burnt beyond recognition. They had opted to have them cremated and their ashes put in decorative boxes.

The boxes were to be buried in the family cemetery alongside the rest of their ancestors. Arthur was in charge of everything. He stood tall, calm, and dignified as he directed everyone with the setup.

"Good Morning Jessica and Timothy. Your grandparents are already in the dining room for breakfast."

"Thank you, Arthur, for everything."

"You are more than welcome."

They entered the dining room and served themselves breakfast from the chaffing dishes filled with various foods Stella had prepared. Arthur was correct when he mentioned her grandparents were already there. Neither seemed to have a voracious appetite. Instead, they both looked at their plate of food and pushed the food around.

Jessica felt a little self-conscious about the amount of food she had on her plate and the speed at which she could devour it all. She hoped nobody noticed. Her grandmother was always overly critical of the amount of food she ate. This time she didn't seem to notice, lost in her own world of grief. It was a relief to Jessica.

She and Timothy were not ready to share their news about expecting the baby yet. With the deaths of her parents, she knew she was not safe, and neither was her unborn child. Part of her though wanted to tell her grandparents just to give them some sense of hope and happiness, despite the loss of her parents, but she knew it was not a good idea.

After breakfast, they all filed into the garden where the decorative boxes sat on pedestals, the flowers sent from people to show their condolences arranged around each one. The chairs in the garden filled up quickly, and they soon filled the garden with mourners who came to pay their final respects.

Richard Jr. joined Jessica and Timothy, sitting in the front row sitting with their grandparents. Jessica couldn't help but think about the day she had met her biological parents and her siblings. It had been a day not unlike today. A day of sorrow and of saying goodbye.

Yet that day had turned into the beginning of her family's reunion and its demise. There were secrets revealed that day. After moving forward to be a family, an unknown entity started to tear them apart.

They thought now that every tragedy, including Alexandria's death, was being orchestrated by the same sadistic serial killer. Samuel was their suspect. As her mind went to him, she looked over her shoulder and saw him sitting a few rows back from them, holding Rita's hand.

As Jessica watched him, she tried to see the cold-hearted killer inside of him. At that moment, though she couldn't, he was gently consoling Rita, squeezing her one hand with his and wiping her tears with his other.

This image of Samuel didn't fit with their summarization of the crimes they felt he committed. She reminded herself that most serial killers seemed normal and fit in with society.

Lena and Steven were there with their daughters, including Danielle, sitting beside Rita. Jessica's gaze scanned them all. The pain and sorrow were so visible on each of their faces. It was at this moment she realized that, although she had an emptiness inside her, their loss seemed so much deeper than her own. They had known her parents for a lifetime; she had known them for a few short months. This made her feel as though she should not be sitting in front and they should be.

The minister startled her out of her thoughts as he started his sermon. The words seemed to float in the surrounding air. They passed through her mind without registering. The familiarity of the funeral service had become so routine that she actually felt numb.

When the minister asked for family and friends to come forward to share stories with the mourners of her parents, it again reminded her of the first time she had met them. The dramatic way in which her father had revealed his true identity.

Jessica hadn't planned on getting up and saying anything, but she found herself getting up and walking to the podium. As she stood there looking out at the mourners, she saw so many now-familiar faces looking at her with sympathy.

"As you all know by now, my name is Jessica Greenhall. I am the daughter of Richard and Mira Gardiner. We all learned that only a few short months ago. After that moment, my family had been trying to mend from years of separation and secrets. Yet tragedy has constantly barraged us. One loss after another."

Jessica paused, looking straight at Samuel.

"Without the love and support of all of you, our friends and family, we could not continue to go on. We thank you all for your support. The senseless loss of our parents so soon after the tragic loss of our brother and sister has rocked my brother Richard and me to our core."

As Jessica continued to lock her gaze on Samuel, he didn't flinch. Either he didn't notice she was looking directly at him, or he didn't care. He showed no reaction to any words she spoke.

"In a couple of short weeks, my fiancé and I will wed in the gardens of the Manor house. That will be the last time I set foot on this cursed island."

Jessica finished and looked at the other remaining two members of the Gardiner family. Jimmy showed such deep sadness. She knew her words hurt him, cut him like a knife. The island was his home. He had given up the love of his life to stay. He didn't know about the child she was carrying, though. Her baby needed her to protect it from the evil on the island. Jessica knew eventually he would forgive her.

Richard Jr. registered a look of understanding. Timothy extended his hand as she sat down next to him. He cradled her in his arms as they sat and listened to more mourners share memories.

The rest of the service seemed to happen in a fog and a blur. When the service finished, they all filled the gardens for a luncheon. Jessica sat and picked at a plate of food absentmindedly.

Rita sat down beside her, placing her hand on Jessica's arm.

"I am so sorry for your loss. Mira was like another daughter to me. I hope you know you will always be welcome to come to visit."

"Thank you, Rita. My mom thought fondly of you as well. I will keep your offer in mind."

Samuel stood behind Rita. Jessica looked up at him. For the first time, she thought she saw a touch of sorrow. It was on the edge of his eyes. *Could he be feeling remorse? Did he not realize the emotional damage the loss of her mother would be to the woman he proclaimed to love?* The thoughts raced through her mind. He broke her thoughts.

"Jessica, I know you and I haven't had a close relationship. I know I haven't always been friendly to you. Please know I am truly sorry for your loss. Your father and mother were gracious and kind people. They didn't deserve the fate dealt them."

As Samuel spoke, almost choked with emotion, Jessica couldn't process the words he was saying with what she knew. She couldn't tip their hand. The rage she felt toward him bubbled up inside of her. It was hard to swallow, but she had to.

"Thank you, Samuel. I hope someday the tides of fate will turn in the Gardiner family's favor."

With those words spoken, she got up and walked away. She was exhausted and just wanted to go take a nap. When she found Timothy, they said goodbye to her grandparents, who were heading home, and then they retreated to their bedroom.

They both fell asleep with their dress clothes on, holding each other tight. It had been an emotional day. Jessica dreamed of their wedding day.

It was beautiful. The weather was sunny with wisps of clouds in the sky. She faced Timothy to exchange their vows, and to her horror, realized blood covered his face. She awakened covered in sweat and shaking. Timothy stirred next to her and woke up with a start when he heard Jessica crying while covering her face with her hands.

Timothy held her close as she recounted the nightmare.

"It's okay. It was just a horrible nightmare. Soon we will be married and we will be free of this place."

"Will we ever really be free of here, though?"

"Yes, remember our plans. We will be free and safe."

There was a knock on the bedroom door, and Timothy got up to see who it was. To his surprise, it was Betty.

"Sorry to bother you both. Ms. Stella has sent me up to tell you dinner will be ready shortly."

"No bother, Betty. Thank you. We will be down momentarily."

"You are welcome. Oh, and I am sorry for your loss, Ms. Jessica."

"Thank you, Betty."

Jessica was still groggy from her nightmare. She didn't know if it was the grogginess or her emotional exhaustion, but she sensed something different about Betty and she couldn't figure out what it was.

Timothy and Jessica changed and got washed up. Then they went down and joined Richard Jr. and Jimmy for dinner. Arthur had already left, and Jessica felt a pang of guilt for not saying goodbye.

As the four of them sat and ate, they kept the conversation light. Jimmy and Richard Jr. had kept their pact not to drink, which helped Jessica not feel obliged to make excuses why she wasn't having any alcohol herself.

Jessica kept staring off and contemplating the events of the day. The interactions she had with people. The oddities of how Samuel's actions and words didn't fit what they thought he did. And that's when it hit her. The difference she noticed in Betty was in her words. Specifically, how she spoke. Her diction was more proper than back-woods, as she had always spoken.

She needed to find Betty and talk to her. Jessica didn't know why this change bothered her so much, but it did. When she got up and left the room, the men were all looking at each other, a bit confused. Especially Timothy. He didn't go af-ter her though because he didn't want the others to suspect anything was wrong with Jessica. He imagined she was having a bout of pregnancy sickness. It did hit her at odd times.

Betty was upstairs cleaning out the guest rooms used the previous night.

"Hi Betty, I hope I am not bothering you or interrupting your work?"

"Hello, Ms. Jessica. No, you are not bothering me. Is there something you need? I can get it for you when I am finished in this room."

"No, no. I don't need anything. I just wanted to ask you something."

Betty froze. She looked at Jessica quizzically.

"What do you need to ask me?"

Jessica didn't know how to ask what she wanted without sounding offensive, but she did anyway.

"I couldn't help but notice a difference in you. You are speaking a bit different from how you usually do."

Betty gave Jessica a smile and shrugged.

"I have been taking speaking lessons. I met a new guy, and I didn't want to seem uneducated."

Jessica paused and felt stupid for having broached the subject at all.

"Oh, that's nice. I am glad you have a boyfriend. I am sorry again for bothering you."

"It's okay, Ms. Jessica. You aren't bothering me one bit."

Jessica went back downstairs and met the men who had moved to the parlor after dinner. She felt ashamed that she had pointed out the change in Betty's speaking. Why shouldn't Betty better herself? Good for her.

CHAPTER ELEVEN

Preparations

T HEY FILLED THE WEEKS leading up to the wedding with the hustle and bustle of final preparations and plans. Everyone welcomed the chaos,
as it filled their minds with happy thoughts and
took their minds off of the intense grief they had
all been feeling for months.

Jimmy was working on making sure security was the tightest it could be. He wanted his
cousin's wedding to go off without a hitch. He
had weekly meetings with Rolly to discuss the
best strategic placement of their manpower. They
knew their threat was Samuel, so they were con-

centrating on keeping their eyes on him at all times.

Melissa had refused Jimmy's invitation to be his date. As much as it bothered him knowing the woman he loved wouldn't step foot on the island, it made him even more determined to catch Samuel and lock him up for good. Then they would be free to live their lives together and pursue their relationship.

Timothy and Jessica had gone back to Connecticut the day after Jessica's parent's funeral. However, they were back on the island helping with the preparations for the wedding, which was coming up on Saturday.

Danielle wanted to take Jessica out for a bachelorette party. Jessica was trying to come up with every excuse in the book not to go out. She didn't want to tell Danielle about the baby. Thankfully, her tiny baby bump really wasn't showing.

"Come on Jess, it's a tradition. We have to take you out. I will drive and not drink, and I will make sure you get home safely."

"Danielle, I appreciate all that you are doing as my maid of honor. I just don't feel up to going out and drinking. I am afraid if I drink, I won't stop."

"Okay, how about we just take you out to dinner, then? No drinking."

Jessica resigned herself to going out just for dinner. At least, then she wouldn't feel obligated to explain why she wasn't drinking.

When Danielle showed up to pick up Jessica, Richard Jr. had answered the door. The awkwardness between the two was palpable in the air. Jessica wished they would just talk and work things out. You could tell they were both miserable without each other. But she also knew the danger they all faced and they couldn't be happy until the danger was gone. Jessica met them in the foyer and gave Timothy a kiss and a hug.

"I won't be out late. See you when I get home. Love you."

"Love you too. Have fun."

As the women drove away, Danielle looked over at Jessica. She envied Jessica's resiliency. If she had gone through everything Jessica had been through in the last six months, she wouldn't be able to keep her composure as Jessica always seemed to.

"How do you do it?"

The odd question startled Jessica.

"Do what?"

"How do you seem so together? So confident of yourself when your entire world is seemingly crumbling around you?"

"What is the alternative? Curl up in a ball and stop living? How would that honor those we have lost?"

"I suppose you are right. You just amaze me. I didn't even have the strength to stay with Richard Jr. through it all."

"He still loves you. You know that, right?"

"Yeah. I still love him too, but I can't. I just can't risk having to watch him die. It would kill me. That's why after your wedding I am moving away. I can't stick around and watch what happens next."

Jessica couldn't believe what Danielle was say-ing. She understood all too well, though. The need and desire to get away and never come back. She and Timothy had discussed it many times. The urge to tell Danielle all about the cottage in Ireland and how they were going to go live there was strong. However, she resolved to keep that to herself.

After they picked up Danielle's sisters, mother, and grandmother, the conversation turned lighter and focused on the upcoming nuptials. The restaurant they went to was fancy, with crystal chandeliers and silk table clothes. Jessica felt a little underdressed. Then Danielle pulled out a bride-to-be sash and a tiara and made her put it on. At least the tiara made her feel more at ease in the restaurant.

Dinner was delicious and the women all enjoyed the festive night out. Jessica abruptly excused herself and hurriedly walked to the ladies restroom. She barely made it into the stall when her entire dinner came back up. There was a quiet tap on the stall door.

"Jess, are you okay?"

It was Danielle.

"Yeah, I am fine. Something I ate didn't sit well, I guess."

As Jessica came out of the stall, Danielle eyed her carefully.

"Are you pregnant?"

"What? No, what gave you that idea?"

"Um, I don't know. A ravenous appetite, not wanting to drink, and now getting sick for no reason."

"I told you it must be something I ate."

Jessica said it with a little more annoyance than she really wanted to. She felt sorry after she did because the look on Danielle's face changed from concern to hurt.

"Okay. I am sorry I mentioned it. I just remember my mom telling me stories about when your mom was pregnant with you and your mom was awfully sick."

The mention of her mom made her close her eyes. She contemplated telling Danielle the truth and then, without warning, Danielle pushed past her and closed the stall door behind her just in time. As she lost all content of her stomach into the toilet.

"Are you okay, Danielle?"

"Yeah, I am fine. As you said, it must be the food."

Both women splashed water on their faces and rinsed out their mouths by cupping the water into their hands and drinking it. They gave each other a smile in the mirror.

When they got back to the table, the others were talking about ordering dessert. Neither of them really wanted to eat another bite after being sick, but they didn't tell the others. They ordered a small slice of carrot cake each, hoping it would stay down.

It wasn't until after Danielle had dropped off her family she mentioned what happened in the bathroom again.

"You know, if you were pregnant, I would understand why you want to keep it a secret. I won't discuss what happened back in the bathroom with anyone else."

Jessica looked at Danielle as she was driving. There was something different about her lately, but she couldn't figure out what it was. She hadn't changed her hair or the style of clothes she wore. It wasn't like Betty, who talked differently. But she was different.

"Well, thank you, but I am not pregnant. I won't tell anyone about what happened in the bathroom either, though. So that you know."

When Jessica got dropped off, Danielle didn't come inside. The guys were hanging out in the parlor playing pool when Jessica entered. Timothy came over and gave her a hug.

"How was your evening?"

Pressing against his chest, her breasts hurt. Another aspect of pregnancy she was becoming accustomed to.

"It was nice. I am tired though, so I am going to bed."

"Do you want me to join you?"

"Nah, you are having fun. Don't stop because of me."

"Okay, if you say so. Love you. Goodnight."

"Love you too."

Timothy kissed Jessica, and she headed upstairs. She couldn't wait to get in bed and go to sleep. She was so tired. That was another aspect of the pregnancy she was getting used to. Being tired all the time. After getting into her pajamas, she quickly fell asleep when her head hit the pillow.

In her dream, she was in the Manor's garden. She was holding a baby, her baby. Happiness filled her heart. When she looked up, Danielle was walking toward her, smiling. She had something in her arms. The realization hit Jessica that Danielle had a baby in her arms. Jessica jolted awake just as Timothy was climbing into bed.

"Are you okay? Another bad dream?"

"Not really a bad dream. Not at all. I was holding our baby."

"Oh, was it that ugly? You startled awake."

"NO. Not at all. It was just we were here in the garden, with the baby."

She didn't want to tell Timothy everything about her dream. About Danielle. She hated lying to him, but she knew if her gut was telling her that

Danielle was pregnant also, it was best nobody knew.

"I can see why that would startle you. We have no plans on bringing the baby here, ever."

"Exactly!"

Timothy climbed into bed and cradled her. They were both soon fast asleep.

CHAPTER TWELVE

Boats and Bad Luck

TIMOTHY WOKE UP, STILL holding Jessica. He didn't want to disturb her; he knew she needed the sleep. Carefully, he extracted himself from their bed. The guys were going fishing instead of having a bachelor party. After getting dressed, he went downstairs to meet the guys for breakfast.

Jimmy and Richard Jr. were engaged in a conversation at the dining room table. They both looked up and paused when Timothy entered the room.

"Are you ready to catch some fish today, Timothy?"

"I already caught the best fish out there, but sure, it's going to be a fun, relaxing day."

"Jessica isn't here right now. No need to suck up, bro."

"I'm not. She is truly the catch of a lifetime for me. Sorry if you guys can't understand that."

Jimmy looked at Richard Jr. They both understood, in more ways than one. Both of them had felt the same about the women they loved.

The men joked around while finishing their breakfast. Just as they were getting up from the table, Jessica entered to have her breakfast.

"Good morning, boys. I am glad I caught you all before you headed out. Enjoy the day. Have fun. And be safe."

Timothy hugged Jessica and gave her a quick peck on the cheek.

"Good morning. We will have fun, but as I told the guys already. I caught the fish of a lifetime."

Jessica smiled and laughed as she watched the guys head out of the Manor house. At that moment, she didn't have a care in the world. All she thought about was in three short days she would marry the love of her life and then leave this island forever.

The guys went to the garage to get some ATVs to ride to the dock. Samuel was in there working on something that had broken. Jimmy was the first to acknowledge him.

"Hey Samuel, you sure you don't want to go fishing with us to celebrate Timothy getting hitched?"

"I don't enjoy fishing out on boats. I used to, but no more."

"Okay, man, but I have a feeling you are going to miss out on some good fun. If you change your mind, just meet us down at the docks. My friend will pick us up there in a half-hour."

"Thanks, but I am good. Besides, I have a lot of work to do around here."

Jimmy had purposefully asked Samuel if he wanted to go for three reasons. First, the guys could monitor him, so they knew Jessica would be safe while they were gone. The second reason was to get more information on Samuel. If Samuel really was Benjamin, it would fit that he used to enjoy fishing on boats, but since the accident no longer enjoyed it. The third reason was if Samuel was Benjamin, then that meant he was Jimmy's biological father and it would be nice to know more about him. Other than he was a complete psychopath.

Richard Jr. led the way with the ATVs down to the docks. As they boarded the boat, they noticed Betty coming out from the galley entrance.

"Good morning fellas, Ms. Stella sent me down here to stock your galley with plenty of food. Thank goodness she did. All that was down there was beer!"

The guys laughed, helped Betty off the boat, thanking her, and got ready to launch on their trip. To all of their amazement, Samuel rode up to the docks at the last minute. As he climbed off the ATV, there was a look of trepidation on his face.

"Is that invitation still open?"

Jimmy, Timothy, and Richard Jr. all looked at each other, still awestruck that he had actually shown up. It was Richard Jr, that spoke up.

"Sure, climb on board. There is plenty of room for one more."

They watched him shakily board the vessel with beads of sweat on his bald head. He wobbled as some small waves rocked the boat gently from side to side. Putting his hands on the rail, he steadied himself and went and had a seat with the others.

Jimmy's friend Robert, who owned the boat, untied from the dock and steered the boat out into Gardiners Bay, heading towards Long Island Sound.

Getting into the Sound, they started casting their lines. Samuel eased into the fishing with the others. His face was pale, and the others could see the visible shake in his hands as he tried to maneuver the rod and reel.

Jimmy observed Samuel. It really seemed that something petrified him about being on the boat. He felt sorry for him and almost forgot that he was the prime suspect in their investigation.

The boat rolled back and forth more when the waves grew bigger. Samuel clumsily put down the fishing gear and went into the galley area of the boat. Jimmy followed him. The door to the head shut behind Samuel and Jimmy heard the retching noises from within. He shook his head, thinking *poor guy* to himself. He grabbed a water and headed back up to the deck, leaving Samuel behind.

It was about a half-hour before Samuel showed his face on the deck again. The paleness of his face was quite obvious to his fellow passengers. He sat down, taking deep breaths of the salty sea air. Slowly, the color returned to his cheeks.

As Jimmy watched though, Samuel's eyes widened as if he was seeing a ghost. Following his gaze, Jimmy saw what he was looking at. There were wisps of smoke coming from the galley area.

"Robert, I think we might have a problem!"

The men jumped into action as the smoke got worse. Samuel froze in his place.

It turned out to be a small electrical fire, but the incident rattled them all enough to call it quits for the day. When they docked the boat, they all sat there eating the food Stella had packed, so it didn't go to waste, except Samuel. He couldn't get off the boat fast enough.

As Jimmy cracked open the first cold beer in weeks, he reflected on what had transpired out on the Sound. He had witnessed a vulnerable side of Samuel. If he had been acting, he should get an academy award.

When the men made it back up to the Manor house, Jessica was sitting in the parlor reading. She placed her bookmark inside the book and set it down as Timothy bent down to give her a kiss.

"How was the fishing trip?"

"Well, it was going well until we had a minor problem."

"What slight problem?"

"A small electrical fire in the galley."

"OMG, are you guys all right?"

"We are all fine. As for Samuel, he looked like he saw a ghost."

"Wait, Samuel went with you all?"

Jimmy and Richard Jr. jumped in to help fill in the details of what happened. Timothy sat down next to Jessica and she wrapped her arms around him, leaning her head on his chest.

"Do you guys think Samuel is responsible for the fire?"

Jimmy shook his head.

"I don't know. It shook him up just as much as it did us. Robert is going to look more closely at the wiring and see if he can determine what happened. At this moment, though, it looks like a freak accident."

"I am just glad you are all okay and safe."

They spent the rest of the night playing pool and just hanging out. Jessica thought about how much she was going to miss this. She loved hanging out with her brother and cousin. Maybe once Samuel was behind bars, she could feel safe coming back. But until then, there was nothing else they could do except plan on staying far away from the island.

Timothy watched his bride-to-be. He could almost read her thoughts just by watching her eyes. They would sparkle when she laughed with her brother and cousin. Then they would dim as her gaze stared off into the distance. He knew she was contemplating their plans. Leaving the only family she had. It was what they needed to do to stay safe, but it would not be easy at all.

Even Timothy felt the pangs of guilt and sorrow creeping over him about the decision they had made. Jimmy and Richard Jr. had become the closest thing to brothers he ever had.

Soon they all were too tired to stay up any later, and they knew the next day would be a busy one. Out-of-town family and friends would come in for the wedding and stay at the Manor house. Jimmy would have last-minute meetings with Rolly and the security crew. Rehearsal would take place and the rehearsal dinner.

As Jessica climbed the stairs, it hit her that was the last time they would sit in the parlor, just the four of them, and a tear rolled down her cheek.

"Are you okay?"

"Yeah, I am fine. Just thinking about everything and everyone. And as much as I hate this place, how much I am going to miss the people here."

"I know Jess, I am too. I am too."

Timothy wrapped his arm around Jessica's shoulder as they walked to their bedroom. It would be the last night they slept together before their wedding. Danielle insisted that the night before the wedding, she and Jessica would have a sleepover. Timothy would take another of the guest rooms.

Jimmy stumbled up the stairs to his bedroom. He was kicking himself for having a few beers. The anxiety rose in his chest. He swept the room and made sure there were no beer cans anywhere. Then he locked his bedroom door and stripped down to his boxers. The bed was comfortable, and he relaxed as he fell asleep.

Richard Jr. hadn't drank as much as Jimmy had. He was monitoring his cousin. The fact he had entrusted him with his past secrets made him feel responsible for looking out for him. After getting into some pajama bottoms, he went out into the hallway and sat across from his cousin's door, keeping watch.

In the morning, Jimmy awakened with a bit of dread. He didn't want to look and see if there were beer cans strewn around, but he did. To his astonishment, there were none. He carefully unlocked his door and opened it to find Richard Jr. fast asleep in the hallway, blocking his bedroom door.

Jimmy smiled, closed the door, and went to take a shower. As the door closed, Richard woke up. His back was sore from lying on the floor all night and his neck was stiff. He heard Jimmy inside his bedroom and the door to the bathroom shut, so he took that as his cue to go get ready for the day as well.

The sun shone into the bedroom where Jessica and Timothy were still sleeping. She rolled over into his arms that were encircling her. Her eyes were still closed, and she nuzzled her face into his chest.

Timothy pulled her tighter against him and slowly opened his eyes. He knew they needed to get up and start their day, but he just wanted a few minutes more of just this. Softly, he kissed her forehead. Her eyes fluttered open, and she looked up at him.

"Are you ready to get this show on the road?"

He looked back at her.

"As ready as I will ever be. How about you?"

Jessica smiled at him.

"Let's do this."

CHAPTER THIRTEEN

Judgement Day

THEY WERE GIDDY WITH excitement. Soon, all their years of planning would pay off. The island would be theirs to have forever and no one would be any the wiser about their hand in it all. It almost seemed too simple.

Everything had fallen into place beautifully in the last six months. They had reserved themselves for the long game years ago and had eventually changed it to a quick game with the turn of events that had occurred at Alexandria's funeral. Now the time had come to finish the job.

They had heard whispers of Jessica and Timothy about a pregnancy. It was the only tidbit of information that was interesting that they had heard in weeks. The family had started discussing more important issues outside the walls of the Manor house. This had become annoying.

Not being able to hear the secrets of the family was infuriating and fueled their anger further. Soon, all the secrets would reveal themselves.

Nobody paid any attention to them, so as the hustle and bustle around the island for the wedding preparations happened, they set up the final grand finale of their plan. The piece de la resistance.

They weren't worried about the cameras since they had invested in a Wi-Fi jammer. By using it, the cameras were inoperable. They could move about The Manor house freely when needed. It had taken them weeks to put everything they needed in place, but it was all there, ready to go.

Tomorrow, their life would change forever. Tomorrow, they would finally have everything they ever desired. It was judgment day for the Gardiner family.

They would have it all, everything they ever wanted and deserved.

CHAPTER FOURTEEN

Sharing Secrets

J ESSICA AND TIMOTHY ENTERED the dining room and were pleased to see that her grandparents were already there. She had been afraid that they would not attend after the deaths of her parents. Alison, Timothy's mother, was also there, and she was chatting with Mr. and Mrs. Kennedy.

Alison beamed as she looked at Timothy. She placed her hand on Mrs. Kennedy's arm and excused herself from the conversation. Sliding out of her chair, she walked up to Jessica and Timothy and hugged them both.

"Ah, there are the bride and groom. We have been waiting for you both to emerge from your bedroom. Stella has prepared a feast for break-fast. Grab some before your cousin Jack gets here. His appetite is monstrous!"

Timothy laughed and followed Jessica over to the sideboard filled with chaffing dishes. He filled his plate, even though his stomach was feeling queasy. The nerves were rattling him the closer they got to the wedding.

He was sure he wanted to marry Jessica. The fact was, he was never so sure about anything in his life. The nerves were not cold feet. It was more about executing their plan after the wedding and catching the serial killer. He prayed they were suc-cessful so they could all resume living a normal life. Timothy pushed those thoughts back into his mind and focused his attention on his bride-to-be.

Jessica filled her plate, which garnered a look of repugnance from her grandmother. Her grand-mother never appreciated her appetite and how much food she ate. While she never actually called her fat. There had been several instances where her grandmother noted women should watch what they ate and remain slender in build. Jessica loved food and while she wasn't exactly overweight, she wasn't slender either. She had her curves, and she was comfortable with her body that she didn't really care what anyone else thought.

At the moment, she was thankful for the curves that hid her pregnancy. She started to worry less about hiding her growing appetite since everyone knew she loved food as well.

Jimmy, Richard Jr., and Arthur joined the others in the dining room. They kept the conversation light and focused on the wedding. There were too many people who were not aware of the danger the family was in to discuss all of that.

Martin escorted Danielle into the dining room. Jessica watched her brother's facial expression. The love he still felt for Danielle was apparent in the way his eyes glistened when he looked at her. She could see the muscles in his shoulders tense as he held himself from going over and pulling her in his arms. The pain her brother was in made Jessica feel guilty about asking Danielle to be her maid of honor.

Danielle's face was soft, but when she looked at Richard Jr., a hint of sadness filled her eyes and her jaw tightened into a set of blank expressions. The tension between the two was still as thick as a dense fog.

"Hey Jess, are you ready to go get our manicures and pedicures?"

"Sure, Danielle. I am just finished eating, anyway. Let me go get my sandals from upstairs."

Jessica had never had a manicure or pedicure in her life, but Danielle had insisted they get them for the wedding. She caved and let her schedule an appointment for them both. As they were leaving, she felt bad about not inviting her grandmother or Timothy's mom, but she noticed the two women chatting it up nicely in the parlor, which gave her a little comfort. She kissed Timothy goodbye and left with Danielle.

The ride to the mainland was short. However, it was just enough time for the two women to talk. Jessica opened up first.

"Danielle, the other day. When we were in the bathroom, and we both got sick. You asked me if I was pregnant. Is that because you are pregnant?"

Danielle looking out the corner of her eye while driving opened her mouth, then closed it. She seemed flustered. Jessica felt bad about asking her. The thought had been nagging at the corner of her mind since she had the dream the other day. Danielle finally responded.

"I am. No one knows. I mean it, no one. I don't want anyone to know, especially Richard. When the wedding is over, I am moving away on Sunday. My parents don't even know. I will call them when I get to where I am going. That, though, will remain a secret. So, what about you? Are you ready to come clean and tell me the truth?"

Jessica took a deep breath in and exhaled. Danielle had confided in her. Should she keep her secret or should she tell her the truth?

"Okay. I am sure you understand why I am keeping it a secret. I promise to keep your secret. Please keep mine. Yes, I am pregnant."

Jessica felt as if it lifted an immense weight off her shoulders, sharing her and Timothy's secret. The rest of the afternoon, the two women giggled and just thoroughly relaxed while being pampered. When they returned to The Manor house, their jubilation continued and carried over to the others.

There was an air of happiness that hung over the island and it gave Jessica hope that their future would not comprise any more tragedy or dark clouds. Timothy's cousin Jack had arrived while they were gone. A mean game of pool consumed the guys in the parlor.

The tension between Danielle and Richard Jr. seemed to ease a little and more than once, Jessica caught the two of them laughing in conversation with one another. She thought about Danielle's secret and wished her brother could know he was going to be a father. He would be a great dad. Unfortunately, she could not tell him and she knew Danielle had no intentions of sharing the information with him.

Jessica glanced outside the window and day-dreamed about a time in the future when they could all be together again. Safe. Where her child and her brother's child could grow up knowing each other. Timothy sat down next to Jessica and whispered in her ear.

"Penny for your thoughts."

"Just daydreaming about the future, my dear."

"Ah, that's why you have such a huge smile on your face."

"Definitely, I am feeling very hopeful that all of our futures will be brighter than the last six months."

Jimmy was the only one that seemed tense. He excused himself from the parlor and took a long walk to the security shack. His mind was stuck on making sure all the security measures they put in place would be enough to keep the family and all their guests safe during the wedding festivities. He just couldn't fathom losing anyone else. If there were any more deaths on his watch, he would feel as though he failed. He couldn't live with that.

He wished Melissa were with him at the moment. Taking out his cell phone, he dialed her number.

"Hey Jimmy, is everything okay? I figured I wouldn't be hearing from you until the wedding was over."

"Yeah, everything is okay. I am just feeling a lot of anxiety about tomorrow. I needed someone I could trust to talk to about it."

"It's normal for you to feel anxious, Jimmy. You have a big job. Sometimes I don't know how you do it. I am sure everything is going to go fine. The wedding will be beautiful and everyone will stay safe."

"I wish I was as confident as you are about this. I don't know why I am so unsure. We have done everything to make sure we keep everyone safe. However, my gut just tells me we can't."

"Jimmy, you got this. When the wedding is over, and everyone leaves the island, you should take a vacation. Come and visit me. You deserve some downtime."

"I will think about it. Thanks for having confidence in me, and for the invite."

After finishing up the conversation with Melissa, Jimmy felt a little more relaxed. The thought of going to see her cheered him up. She wanted to be with him, just not on the island. He understood. The thought of leaving the island for good was starting to be enticing. Maybe Jessica and Timothy had the right idea. Leaving the island for good.

They were planning on leaving the island and not coming back, at least not until they caught Samuel. Jimmy didn't know if he could leave his adoptive parents behind. He would have to sit down with them and discuss the possibility of them all moving off the island, as Melissa had with her parents.

Then there was Richard Jr. How could he leave him with the sole responsibility of the island? Everyone he loved was dead or leaving. He couldn't add to that burden on his cousin. They had become close in the last few months. Almost like brothers.

As Jimmy walked back to The Manor house, he noticed Rita's car parked next to Samuel's truck. Seeing it made Jimmy relax a little. Samuel would be busy entertaining Rita, hopefully too busy to kill any of them. Although she had been with him the weekend of the fatal fire.

Everyone was still in the parlor having a fun time. Richard Jr. walked up to Jimmy and put his hand on his shoulder.

"Come, let me beat you in a game of pool. It might take your mind off your worrying."

"What makes you think I am worried?"

"The lines on your forehead, man. They are deeper than the grand canyon."

Jimmy laughed and grabbed a pool stick while Richard Jr. racked the balls.

"I guess beating you would be fun and would clear my mind."

Jessica and Danielle said goodnight to the rest of them and headed upstairs to bed. They were both exhausted, and they knew the next day would be full of a barrage of emotions.

Tomorrow, she and Timothy would become husband and wife. Their lives together would start. Tomorrow, their future would be hopeful.

CHAPTER FIFTEEN

The Wedding

IT WAS THE MORNING. The sunshine was bright through the windows. As the dust danced in the sunbeam, Jessica opened her eyes. Danielle was awake already and was busying herself organizing the girl's dresses. They knew they needed to go downstairs and get their breakfast. The hairdresser and the make-up artist would be at the Manor house in a short period.

Both of them gathered themselves in their robes labeled Bride and Maid of Honor and went down to the dining room. None of the guys were awake, yet it seemed. They didn't know what time they had eventually gone to bed.

They filled their plates and then took trays of their food up to the bedroom to eat. When they were done, they called down to the kitchen to have Stella send Betty up to get the trays.

Betty knocked on the door. Jessica opened it.

"Ms. Stella sent me up to grab the trays."

"Of course. Here they are. Thank you, Betty."

"You are going to be a beautiful bride, Ms. Jessica."

"Thank you, Betty. Maybe someday soon your new guy will make you his beautiful bride."

"Maybe. That would be nice."

Betty smiled as she left Jessica and Danielle to get ready.

Martin escorted the photographer, the hairdresser, and the make-up artist up to Jessica's room. A flurry of activity began as they prepared the girls for the wedding.

The men were congregating and preparing in Timothy's room. They had brought a photographer up to take pictures of them preparing.

When Jessica's hair and make-up were complete, the photographer wanted to take some photos of her looking at her dress. Looking at it, emotions washed over Jessica. She struggled to blink back the tears as she remembered Samantha picking it out and both of them falling in love with it.

The photographer caught a single tear escaping from Jessica's eye. It made a beautiful picture. The make-up artist, though, was fraught with anxiety.

"No, no. Do not cry! You will mess up your beautiful make-up."

Danielle caught the make-up artist's hand and calmly explained the situation.

"Ma'am. Her sister, who passed away a few months ago, picked out that dress. There are bound to be some tears. I am sure the job you did can weather the potential storm."

"Oh, I am so sorry, ma'am. I didn't know. My deepest condolences."

"Thank you. It's okay, you didn't know. I will try not to shed any more tears."

When Danielle's hair and make-up were complete, it was time for the women to have some

more before pictures taken together. The photographer posed the two girls for various shots and
they all laughed as Jessica made silly faces. She
was used to being on the other end of the lens and
she was feeling self-conscious.

Then it was time to slip into their dresses. It dis-
mayed Jessica that her dress was slightly tighter
than it had been at her last fitting, although it still
fit. Danielle had the same issue.

Neither of them mentioned it, even though they
both knew why the dresses had become snug.
They smiled a knowing smile at each other and
left it at that. The photographer took more pictures and then ushered both women down into
the gardens to take some more pictures before
the guests arrived.

Jessica and Timothy had opted not to have a
first-look picture taken before the wedding. They
both wanted to have their first look at each other
as Jessica walked up the aisle. The photographers
had made sure they would position themselves in
the right place to catch both of their faces.

Soon, it was time for the ceremony to begin. Jessica's palms were sweating as she picked up her bouquet to hold while walking down the aisle. She gently slid her hand over the charm bracelet fastened to her bouquet that held pictures of her mother, father, sister, and brother. They were with her in spirit and she choked back the tears, remembering the promise she had made upstairs.

The music started and Danielle walked through the gardens in front of Jessica, to the gazebo where the minister stood waiting in the center. Timothy was standing to the right and next to him was Richard Jr. Her heart ached. She wished she could tell Richard she was carrying his child. The thought of them being able to marry each other someday flashed through her mind. She knew it could not happen until the serial killer was found and caught.

When she got to the gazebo, she took her place and turned to watch Jessica walk down the aisle. Arthur and Jimmy escorted her. The smile that spread across Jessica's face as she saw Timothy waiting for her melted Danielle's heart. That was true love. Love that wasn't afraid to face danger in the eye. She wished she had that courage.

Timothy's breath hitched as he got his first glimpse of Jessica. He wiped his eyes as a few tears slipped out. She was stunningly beautiful. He already knew this, but seeing her with her hair pulled up on the top of her head with a ring of baby's breath and little ringlets of her red hair framing her face, just emphasized it. Now he knew why she and Samantha had fallen in love with this dress. It was perfect for Jessica.

When Jessica reached Timothy, they faced each other as the minister began the ceremony. It all seemed like a dream, except in this one everything went as planned and there was no blood. Jessica was relieved when they exchanged their vows and they were pronounced husband and wife. Her nightmares had not come to fruition, thankfully.

They both seemed to relax more when the afternoon festivities began. While they sat at the head table, they could see Samuel with his date, Rita. Rolly was sitting at the same table, conversing and acting as though he was just another wedding guest.

The wedding guest list was small and many of the guests were coming up to the head table and congratulating the newlyweds. Lena and Steven made their way up as well.

"Oh Jessica, you look as beautiful as your mom did on her wedding day. I know she is smiling down at you."

"Thank you, Lena. I feel her presence today too. Thank you for coming."

As the evening went on with no incident, Jessica and Timothy loosened up. They danced to their hearts' content and felt truly happy.

Just as the evening was coming to a close, the DJ made an announcement.

"The bride and groom would like to thank all of you for being a part of their special day. Now, if everyone could bring their chairs to the open area of the Gardens, we will conclude the festivities with a fireworks display."

Jessica and Timothy sat side by side with Richard Jr. and Danielle flanking each of them.

With a sideways glance, Jessica saw that Rita and Samuel were sitting to the side of Danielle and slightly behind, while Rolly was sitting directly behind them.

Jessica was relieved to see Rolly still closely monitoring Samuel. It made her feel the safest she had felt in months. She clasped Timothy's hand in hers and leaned her head on his shoulder as they prepared to watch the display.

Jimmy had excused himself from the festivities under the tent to go supervise the fireworks display to be set off. He was feeling lighter than he had in a long time. The stress of the last few months seemed to wash away as the day progressed without a single incident.

Maybe they had been wrong, maybe their grief had turned to paranoia and there really was no serial killer. All the deaths might have been accidents. Maybe their grief had led them all on a wild goose chase. The pyrotechnicians started the display and Jimmy watched wistfully.

Back at the gardens, the lights went out as the fireworks display started. The guests oohed, aahed, and clapped their hands. The bursts of red, green, blue, and purple lit up the night sky.

Timothy squeezed Jessica's hand and as she looked over at him with her eyes sparkling with happiness, the grand finale started. The booms were loud and startled Jessica.

Timothy dropped Jessica's hand and in the flash of the bursts, Jessica saw him clutch his chest. His white suit turned red. He looked down and then looked at her. She went to scream and as she did; she felt the searing pain in her own back. Jessica looked down and realized she was also bleeding. She turned and grabbed Danielle's arm as her vision went dark.

Danielle was enjoying the light display as she felt a firm hand on her arm. To her horror, realizing it was Jessica who was bleeding from a wound on her back through to her front. The hand let go just as Jessica collapsed to the ground. Danielle looked over at Timothy, slumped in his chair, bleeding as well. And then her eyes went to Richard Jr. lying on the ground with a wound to the head. She screamed as the grand finale finished and everyone went silent.

Chaos ensued as the security team and Rolly called for medical help to the island and herded the guests into the grand room in the Manor house. Rolly was determined not to let anyone leave.

As the grand finale finished, Jimmy felt content that the evening had gone as planned. It surprised him when one of his security team members came riding up on his ATV, looking distraught.

"Boss, we have been trying to reach you on your radio."

Jimmy went to reach for his radio and realized he had left it on his ATV parked fifty feet away. His gut wrenched.

"What happened? Why are you trying to reach me?"

"There has been a shooting."

"Oh, my God. Who was shot?"

"Jessica, Timothy, and Richard Jr."

Jimmy's heart sank as he ran toward his ATV. He heard the crackle of the radio and the frantic voices on the other end. He slipped his radio on his belt. As he started up the machine, something rattled off the front of it he hadn't seen before. It was a drone controller. He did not know what it was doing there. He picked it up and secured it, then headed back to the Manor house and the gardens.

Rolly met Jimmy in the gardens.

"It wasn't Samuel. I had my eyes on him the entire night. Especially during the fireworks display."

"Where are Jessica, Timothy, and Richard?"

"We have transported them to the open field, awaiting life flights. It's bad Jimmy, I doubt if they are going to make it."

Jimmy crumpled to the ground, holding his head in his hands. Rolly was trying to help him up and console him when one of his detectives approached.

"Serg, We think we found something inside the house."

Jimmy jumped up and tried to compose himself. They followed the detective back to the house.

Jimmy's stomach tightened as the detective led them upstairs and then down the hallway. They stopped at Jimmy's bedroom. Confusion spread over Jimmy's face.

The detective opened the door. Rolly looked inside and then looked at Jimmy.

"Whose bedroom is this?"

Jimmy stood there looking at his room. It was his room, but the stuff in it he had never seen before. There was a birdcage with crows. A jar on his dresser had something floating inside that he recognized as a deer's heart. And sitting on his bed was a drone with a gun strapped to it. His window was wide open with a slight breeze blowing the curtains.

"Mine. But I swear I have never seen this stuff before."

Rolly looked at his friend. He was just as perplexed. Then he looked at his detective.

"Is the drone controller in here also? Anyone could have done this."

It was Jimmy that answered, not Rolly's detective.

"I have it. Or I think I do. It was on my ATV when I was coming back. I swear, bro, I didn't do this!"

Rolly looked at Jimmy with a pained expression on his face.

"You know what I have to do, right? I can't just ignore all this evidence because we are friends."

"I know."

Jimmy stuck out his hands and let Rolly handcuff him.

The gasps and murmurs of the guests being allowed to leave after being interviewed echoed in Jimmy's ears as Rolly escorted him into a waiting police cruiser.

CHAPTER SIXTEEN

Chaos

JESSICA SLIPPED IN AND out of consciousness, never opening her eyes. She could hear sirens and voices. She felt the pressure of hands on her. All she could think of was Timothy and their unborn child. Would any of them survive?

Timothy heard voices, and felt hands on him, but also could not open his eyes. He thought about how the most perfect day in his life had now turned into the worst.

"This one is DOA. Let's call the coroner's office. The other two are critical. We need those birds ASAP."

Jessica's mind raced. DOA, she struggled to remember what that stood for. Then it hit her, dead on arrival. Someone was dead. God NO. She knew it wasn't her, although she knew she was clinging to life by a thread. Please don't let it be Timothy. Then she felt guilty for thinking of her husband first. Please do not let it be Richard Jr. or OH God, please not Danielle and her baby!

Timothy heard the words DOA, and he panicked, thinking he had lost the love of his life and their unborn child. He hadn't kept them safe. The promise he made to keep them safe, was broken.

Danielle was in the grand hall of the Manor house with the other guests being looked over by medical personnel that had been called to the island. They were watching her for shock. Her parents hovered over her.

"I am fine. I just want to know if Richard Jr. and the others are okay."

Lena held onto her daughter's hand and looked imploringly at the medical personnel. They wouldn't look her in the eye.

"I am sure they are going to be okay."

"Mom, there was so much blood. How can they be okay? Especially Richard? It was coming from his head."

Danielle burst into tears and started shaking. The medical personnel convinced her to go to the hospital for observation.

Allison sat holding Jack's hands as the police interviewed them both. She was trembling. The thought of losing her only son after finding him was overwhelming. When they were told they could leave, her first thought was to go to where they brought Timothy. But she did not know where that was.

"What hospital were Timothy and Jessica brought to?"

The officer told her, and then Jack and Allison headed straight to the hospital.

Jessica vaguely remembered being placed in the helicopter and transported to the hospital. She would hear voices and then things would go dark and silent again.

This time, she recognized two of the voices as Arthur and Allison. There were beeps and other sounds that she recognized as hospital-related. She tried to move, but couldn't. Her eyes would not open either.

"They are keeping her sedated. A medically in-duced coma. They have stabilized her. But they can't do anything more until she gets stronger."

"What about Timothy? What about my son?"

"Let's go out in the hall. They say there is a pos-sibility she can hear us. It's best we discuss other things out of earshot."

NO! Jessica shouted in her mind. She wanted to hear about Timothy. Was he alive or dead? A tiny tear trickled out of the corner of her eye and ran down her cheek onto the pillow.

Jimmy sat in the cell at the police station. Rolly had put him in his own cell instead of the general holding cell. They would arraign him on one count of murder and two counts of attempted murder in the morning. More than likely, with the severity of the charges and the rest of the case that might build against him with the evidence found in his room, it was likely that they would set no bail.

If that occurred, he would wind up being transferred to an actual prison. He was terrified.

Despite all of his previous doubts about himself, he knew he didn't do this. There was no way. He had not touched a drop of alcohol all day. His memory of the day's events was crystal clear.

Arthur awoke the next day dreading what needed to be done. He had to gather all the inhabitants of the island and give them the news. There would be a lot of questions. What would happen to them and the island?

He picked up Allison, and they drove to the island together. The inhabitants all gathered inside the Manor house and waited for Arthur to start speaking.

"Good morning everyone, thank you for gathering here. I wish I had good news to share, but unfortunately, I don't. Richard Jr. was pronounced dead on the scene last night. While Jessica and Timothy both succumbed to their injuries in the early morning hours."

Gasps went through the inhabitants, and they could hear sobs throughout the room. Someone asked the first question.

"What does that mean for us?"

"Good question. I will try to answer it. As you know, they have arrested our own Jimmy Driscoll for the murders. What you all do not know is he is the last living heir to the Gardiner estate."

Everyone's eyes went wide. Hands flew up over mouths and rumbles of, "*But how?*" went through the crowd.

"He is the son of the late Mary Gardiner and her lover, Benjamin Timmons. Benjamin was Richard Sr.'s half-brother. He was a Gardiner by birthright."

As Arthur stated this, he looked squarely at Samuel. Samuel's reaction was one of absolute shock. Arthur thought he saw a shimmer of tears in his eyes. Samuel left the room and Arthur continued.

"This is the motive the police think propelled Jimmy to commit these crimes. He was aware he was a Gardiner, and he wanted it all for himself."

"My boy didn't do this!"

It was Stella, and she was looking furious.

"Stella, I understand your feelings. We are all in shock, too. The police have overwhelming circumstantial evidence pointing to Jimmy. I wish it wasn't so. We are going to get him the best defense attorney around. Allison and I will take over operations of the island and the business until we sort things out with Jimmy. For now, you all remain employed."

A collective sigh went through the room. Many of the inhabitants left the room mumbling to themselves and shaking their heads.

Arthur left the island and headed to the courthouse where Jimmy was awaiting his arraignment. He could get a few minutes to talk to him.

"Hey Jimmy, how are you holding up?"

"Not good Arthur. I did not do this. Swear to God. I know it looks bad and all. Samuel must be framing me."

"I don't think it was Samuel. When I gave the news to everyone who you really were, he seemed convincingly shocked and upset."

"Then who could it be, Arthur? Who wants me to go down for this?"

"I don't know, kid. That is the biggest question. I have to tell you, though, what you are being charged with."

"Lay it on me."

"You are being charged with 3 counts of murder in the first degree. They are also investigating whether you could have done the other deaths."

"Jessica, Timothy, and Rich are dead? They are pinning me for everything?"

"Yes, I am sorry. They are trying to. I have a colleague though. He is the best defense attorney around. He will be here shortly to talk to you. We are going to fight this."

"Okay Arthur, thanks."

Arthur left the room and Jimmy waited for the guard to bring him back to the courthouse holding cell. Instead, the guard came in and said he had another visitor. Jimmy assumed it was the defense attorney that Arthur had told him about.

When Samuel walked into the room, Jimmy froze, looking at him. Was he here to finish him knowing he was a Gardiner now, too? Jimmy thought of yelling to the guards. Samuel sat down in the chair across the table from Jimmy and rested his head in his hands.

"My boy."

The tears spilled from Samuel's eyes freely as he continued speaking to Jimmy.

"I always hoped I would get to know you. To know how you grew up and who you became. I didn't know I watched you grow up on the island. And I didn't know it was you. Did your mother know? Did she know I was a Gardiner because I sure as hell didn't know?"

"Ms. Mary, my mother didn't know until the day she died. As I had not known either until Ms. Alexandria told us on her deathbed. So we were right. You are Benjamin, my father."

"Yes, I am. I barely survived the boating accident with my life. When I saw Mary afterward, I tried to tell her who I was so many times, but I couldn't come clean with her and she never realized it was me. Too much of my outward appearance had changed."

"Does anyone else know who you really are?"

"No. Why?"

"I am being framed. I thought it was by you. We suspected that you might be the only other unknown heir to the Gardiner estate. It made sense it would be you picking the family members off one by one."

"You mean to tell me the other deaths weren't accidents?"

"No, we do not believe so. And now I am being pegged for them all. I didn't do this. You need to keep it a secret that you are a Gardiner and you are alive. Can you do that?"

"I will do what needs to be done to help clear your name, kid."

"Thanks, Dad, it's okay for me to call you that, right?"

"Sure, Kid."

Before Samuel left, he gave Jimmy a quick hug. His mind was still spinning at the revelation that all this time he was a Gardiner. If he had known that so many years ago, so much would have been different.

Jimmy resolved to not tell anyone about his conversation with Samuel. He didn't know who he could trust. He felt, though, in every fiber of his being, that Samuel had not known that he was his son or that he was a Gardiner.

Jimmy met with the defense attorney, Mr. Devine. He would enter a not-guilty plea. The attorney assured him they would do everything in their power to get him out on bail, but considering the charges, it was unlikely.

The arraignment went as expected. They charged him with three counts of first-degree murder and had no bail set. They ordered him to be detained while awaiting trial. His attorney attempted to get him to be released to attend the funeral of his cousins, but the judge would not allow it. This was a devastating blow to Jimmy. He could not say goodbye to Jessica, Richard, or Timothy.

Arthur, who had been sitting in the courtroom, left to go back to his office. There was so much to do. He had the funerals to arrange. Out of loyalty and devotion to Alexandria, he would continue to help the family and see Jimmy through his trial. However, he was thinking retirement was sounding pretty good.

When he sat at his desk and opened his mail, there was an envelope with no return address and no stamp. He brought it to his secretary's attention.

"Where did this envelope come from?"

"A courier dropped it off, sir."

Sitting back down at his desk, he opened it and found a birth certificate. The names of the father and mother surprised him, along with the name of the child. This opened up a whole new headache. He knew he had to tread lightly with this information. It had to be authenticated, and he had to have a DNA test done.

He didn't want to place another person in danger. Another previously unknown heir. He had phone calls to make and appointments to set up if the person was willing. This changed a lot of things. And in the back of his mind, he questioned if this person had been behind everything. It seemed unlikely. He couldn't imagine them being a serial killer. Just another pawn in the never-ending game of chess being played with the family.

CHAPTER SEVENTEEN

Perfect Timing

EXCITEMENT PUMPED THROUGH THEIR veins! They had executed their plan flawlessly. Jimmy was sitting in jail, rotting for the crimes they committed. No one suspected them. It had been so easy to get everything into place. They had stored all the evidence pointing to Jimmy in the attic and, while everyone was busy at the wedding, they moved it into his room. The fact the family had been so focused on Samuel as the one targeting them made it easier to set up Jimmy, too.

The old buffoon was grumpy and was in the same spots as them and Jimmy during the crimes. It was great that the family focused on him.

Using the gun attached to the drone to kill the remaining family members worked so effortlessly. Placing the remote on Jimmy's ATV while they used their smartphone to control it worked perfectly.

Now all they had to do was wait for Arthur to get his mail and come find them. Of course, they will act shocked. The years of the drama club and high school theatre really paid off. It was all part of their master plan.

One more funeral, then they would claim their stake in the family estate. When the courts proclaimed Jimmy guilty and then sentenced him to death. They will become the sole living heir. They will have it all. It was perfect.

As they sat there, their phone rang. Looking at the caller ID, they saw it was Arthur. Right on cue.

CHAPTER EIGHTEEN

Big Revelations

ARTHUR SAT WITH THE DNA test results in front of him. They confirmed indeed there was another Gardiner. He shared the information with the police and Jimmy's defense attorney even though he doubted this person had committed any of the crimes they accused Jimmy of committing. He would discuss the results later that day with the person after the funeral.

He was sad that Jimmy could not say goodbye to his cousins properly. He visited Jimmy the day before to let him know what the results were. Jimmy had been just as astonished and also could not fathom that person committing any crimes.

Arthur showed up early on the island to make sure they set up everything for the funerals. Jessica and Richard's grandparents had arrived. They had refused to stay at the Manor house and were determined to leave as soon as their grandchildren were in the ground.

They lay Richard out in a tan coffin with white satin inlaid. They cremated Jessica and Timothy per their wishes. Their remains were inside two beautiful decorative boxes. Flowers adorned the casket and arrangements surrounded the boxes from loving friends and family mourning the losses of the three young adults.

Danielle was early. She went up to Richard's casket to have a private moment with the body of the man she loved. As she said her goodbyes to him, the tears slid down her cheeks and landed on his. In her mind, she vowed to keep their child safe. Unbeknownst to her family, she had packed up many of her belongings that morning and placed them in her car. She planned on leaving right after the funeral.

It was a beautiful funeral service, and it went by quickly. As Danielle left, she headed for the open road off Long Island and to her new beginning. She would call her family when she stopped for the night. There was no definitive plan on where she would end up. She just planned on driving as far away as possible.

Samuel lingered a bit at the graves. He looked at all the past ancestor's headstones. Realizing they were mostly family he never knew he had was overwhelming to him. He hadn't shared with Rita the information that Jimmy and he had discussed. She just assumed he was as shocked and devastated as the rest of them still were.

Everyone seemed like they were in a fog and few stayed long afterward for the luncheon. Arthur sought the person he needed to speak to.

When he found them, he ushered them into another room where they could speak privately.

"Good Afternoon. Do you want me to call you Beatrice or Betty?"

"Either is fine with me. However, I believe Beatrice is a more dignified name. If you are speaking to me privately, this must mean you have the DNA results."

"Yes, Beatrice. I do have the results. It seems you are, in fact, a Gardiner. But, I must warn you. Even though the police have arrested Jimmy. I am not convinced he is the one responsible for the murders. I am worried about your safety."

"Oh my. That is a lot to swallow. I know when you called me the other day and told me of the birth certificate, I assumed it was some sick joke."

"It is no joke. It seems you are Alexandria's half-sister. You had no clue you were a Gardiner?"

"No sir, I had no clue who my daddy was. My Momma, God bless her soul, was very promiscuous. She told me she didn't know who my daddy was."

"Well, with Jimmy in jail and his fate unknown, you are the only surviving heir. You may live in the Manor house. You also will sit in on the business board meetings. We will help mentor you, Allison and I."

"So I can live in the Manor house? Am I expected to still do my housekeeping duties like Jimmy continued to do his security duties?"

"Yes, you can live in the house. No, they will not expect you to do the housekeeping duties. We will hire a new housekeeper. The only reason Jimmy continued to work security was to keep up appearances he was not a Gardiner. Do you want to keep your heritage a secret?"

"That is a lot to think about. I suppose if I move into the house I will need to tell that I am a Gardiner. I guess I am okay with that. That means I will take my chances, but I am sure the security team will keep me safe."

"Well, I guess that is settled, then. I will call a meeting of everyone on the island once all the mourners have left. We will tell them your news and then you can move into the house."

"Thank you, Arthur."

Beatrice left the room. When she was in the foyer, she ran her hands over the furniture and the pictures on the walls. It was all hers. It was hard to contain her happiness. She finally had everything she had always wanted. What she had worked so hard for. Poor Arthur was worried about her safety. How sweet.

Little did he know she was the safest Gardiner ever. She was the mastermind behind it all. The best part was no one suspected her. Poor little Jimmy, taking the fall for everything she did. That was the icing on the cake.

Her hand trailed along the banister as she slowly went upstairs. Now to choose her bedroom. Which room suited her best? She opened the door to Ms. Mary's room, and she remembered her performance screaming as she found Ms. Mary. The memory made her laugh. She should get an academy award for that performance.

This room would be perfect. She would claim it as her own and have all of Ms. Mary's things removed. She would also restore the parlor to its previous glory. No pool table belonged in an elite manor house.

After all the mourners left the island, Arthur wrangled the inhabitants for a meeting. The room was abuzz, not knowing why they were being called together.

"Good evening everybody, thank you for coming on such short notice. I know we are all tired. It's been a long and emotional day for us all. I have some developing news though to share with all of you. It came to my attention anonymously that there was another potential living Gardiner heir besides Jimmy."

Samuel stiffened. He trusted Jimmy not to tell anyone. Jimmy asked him not to say anything, either. He looked on in fear that his secret was about to be revealed.

"Beatrice Adeline Smith, better known as Betty to us all. She apparently did not know who her father was. According to her original birth certificate that she never saw, her father was Alexandria's father as well. I have confirmed this with DNA testing. We have discussed her role as a Gardiner. She will learn the family business and she wants to live in the Manor house. We will look for a new housekeeper to take her previous position."

Samuel relaxed. It wasn't him. His secret was safe. But, Betty. Betty was a Gardiner as well. That was something he could not believe.

Murmurs and whispers ran around the room. Stella eyed Betty suspiciously. Everyone was completely in disbelief at what they were just told. Betty heard someone whisper, "The Gardiner men surely didn't know how to keep it in their pants."

Betty ignored the comment but thought to herself. If they only knew how true that statement was.

Samuel eyed Betty. She appeared as if all of this was news to her. He needed to see Jimmy and tell him what had happened. Maybe this could open up leads into the case. Who knew how many other Gardiner heirs were out there? Others may actually live on the island too, just like Betty. They may need to test every single person on the island to determine their lineage and see if there are any more unknown Gardiners. However, that would mean revealing his secret.

That was something he would have to think about. He knew the accusations against him implicating him in the murders of Alexandria's family. Was he willing to give up his present life to atone for the sins of his past?

Betty was reveling in the astonishment of her fellow inhabitants at her good fortune. There were a few snide comments, of course, especially about her mother. Nevertheless, she took it all in stride, knowing full well she had all the control in the world now.

"Congratulations Betty, Let me know what your favorite meals are since I will be cooking for you regularly."

Stella had approached Betty. She didn't trust what was going on, maybe because her only child was sitting behind bars for a crime he didn't commit.

"Oh, thank you, Stella. Please call me Beatrice from now on, though. This is such a whirlwind surprise. When Mr. Arthur called me up, I did not know what he was talking about. I will let you know tomorrow about my favorite dishes. I eat breakfast early. By five o'clock in the morning, if that's okay with you."

"That is fine. I will have a variety of breakfast foods ready for you in the morning. Do you need help to move your things into the Manor house? I am sure my husband can get some of the men to help."

"Sure, that would be helpful. We can do that tomorrow, though. I think today has been tiring enough for all."

"That's for sure. Just be careful and watch your back. You don't want to end up like my Jimmy or the other Gardiners."

Betty narrowed her eyes at Stella.

"Is that some sort of threat?"

"Why no! I am just worried about your safety with everything that has happened."

"I am sure I will be fine."

The next morning, Samuel set off to visit Jimmy. Stella was up early cooking Betty breakfast and Betty was already making plans for changes at the Manor house. Arthur had given her a charge card connected to the business until they could get one of her own.

When the guards came to get Jimmy for visitation, he had been staring up at the ceiling, wondering how he had gotten himself into this mess. If he had left the island when Melissa asked him to, he wouldn't be sitting in jail. He was the convenient scapegoat.

He wasn't expecting a visitor today, so it surprised him to see Samuel on the other end of the glass holding onto the telephone.

"So what brings you to see me? Should I call you Samuel, Benjamin, or Dad?"

"You can call me whatever you want, son. I am here because there was a big revelation after the funeral yesterday. It turns out there is another Gardiner heir besides me. It's Betty. Betty is Ms. Alexandria's half-sister."

"What? That's crazy!"

"Yeah, it got me thinking. How many other secret Gardiners are out there, especially living on the island? It seems the Gardiner men weren't very faithful, and they were prolific at multiplying."

"You have a valid question. How do you suppose we find that answer?"

"We could have your defense attorney subpoena everyone on the island to submit to a DNA test. If there are more heirs, then there could be enough reasonable doubt to get you set free."

"But that would mean revealing who you are, Dad. I can't ask you to do that. I know what that means."

"If it means clearing you, I would do it. I did what I did years ago because I wanted revenge. Revenge for having to give you up and pretend you died. Ms. Alexandria had no right to force us to give you up. However, your mother wanted the Gardiner fortune, and I loved her so much, I would do anything for her."

"I will talk to my attorney about it. Your name won't be mentioned. I will just say I thought that there could be other heirs and see what he thinks."

"At least you are safe inside these walls."

"Yeah, I guess. You don't think Betty is behind all this, do you? I can't see her being a serial killer."

"I don't know. Time will tell."

CHAPTER NINETEEN

Disappearing

DANIELLE'S EYES WERE GETTING heavy. She had been driving for nearly eight hours, with a few bathroom breaks. Her intentions were to get as far away as possible before she stopped for the night. The motel parking lot she pulled into was semi-full.

As she walked up to the front desk, the frumpy woman with spectacles hanging off the tip of her nose looked her up and down.

"What can I do for you, dear?"

"I would like to rent a room for a couple of days."

"It is sixty-nine dollars a night, dear. So how many nights will you be staying?"

"At least two. Can I let you know tomorrow if it will be longer?"

"Sure, dear."

The woman took the cash Danielle handed her and gave her the change and the key to her room. When Danielle opened the door to the room, the smell of stale air, mustiness, and cigarette smoke filled her nostrils. She opened the windows and left the door open as she unpacked her things from her car.

It was a small room with one double bed, a desk with a chair, a bureau that served double duty as a TV stand, and a small refrigerator. She lifted the sheets and checked for bedbugs. Peering into the bathroom, it was cleaner than she expected, which impressed her. This would have to do. For now, she was too tired to go any further. She had made it to somewhere in Pennsylvania.

It was late, almost midnight by the time she settled in. She needed to call her parents. They had called and texted her multiple times. Guilt crept over her. She didn't want to worry them, but she needed to get as far away as possible before she contacted them. Taking a deep breath, she dialed her mom's cell phone. Her mom picked it up after the first ring.

"Danielle, where are you? We have been worried sick."

"I am okay, mom. I need space, though, and time."

"Honey, I know losing Richard Jr. and the others is hard on you, but you don't need to deal with it all on your own."

"Yes, I do, Mom. In time, you will understand why I left."

"Where are you, though?"

"I am safe, and that is all that you need to know right now. I am sorry."

"Danielle, I don't understand. Why can't you tell us where you are?"

"I am sorry, Mom, truly I am. This is just as hard for me, but this is the only way to ensure you all stay safe and I stay safe."

"You are scaring me, Danielle. Please tell me what is going on."

"I don't mean to scare you. In time, I will let you know what is going on and why I had to leave but now is not the time. Love you, Mom."

"We love you too, Danielle."

She hung up as she heard her mom choke back the tears. Danielle knew this was crushing her. The guilt kept creeping over her. She pushed it out of her mind as she placed her hands on her belly.

Danielle needed sleep. She pulled back the covers to the bed and put her head on the lumpy pillow. Closing her eyes, she saw Richard's lifeless body in the casket. The tears came, and she cried herself to sleep.

In the morning, she showered and then went to find some breakfast. The little diner she found a mile down the road seemed to be the only place she could find. When she stepped through the doors, she felt transported back in time. It reminded her of the old diners she saw in the movies of the fifties and sixties. It had black and white tiled floors and round red covered seats at the chrome-colored counter. There were a few booths, and some tables scattered throughout.

There was a petite waitress taking a customer's order behind the counter and another, more plump waitress taking orders from a table. Danielle chose a table in the corner. She felt out of place here. There was a difference in what the customers were wearing compared to what she was used to. More rugged. Yet, the people all seemed happy and friendly.

She watched as the plump waitress came over to her table.

"Hey there honey, my name is Selma. I will be your waitress this morning. What can I get you to drink while you are looking over the menu?"

"I will have a glass of water and a large orange juice, please."

"Sure thing."

Selma seemed nice. She was back in a flash with the water and orange juice. Danielle placed her breakfast order and watched as more customers filed in. The two waitresses seemed to work well together, taking everyone's orders. They were busy. This gave her a brilliant idea. She thought maybe they could use an extra hand.

When Selma brought her plate and set it down, Danielle thought it was a perfect opportunity to ask.

"Are you looking for any waitresses?"

"Actually, yes. We are down two. They got up and quit yesterday. You got any experience?"

"As a matter of fact, I do! I am looking for a job. I just pulled into town last night."

Selma tilted her head and eyed Danielle.

"Why'd you pick here?"

"I just stopped for the night, but I think I like it here and want to stay awhile."

"Where are you coming from?"

"Long Island, NY."

"What brings you all the way out here?"

"My best friend died, and I needed a change of scenery. Too many memories back home."

Selma's eyes softened, and she put her hand on Danielle's arm.

"I am sorry for your loss. I will bring you an application and I am sure Wendy and Bruce will look it over and want to interview you."

"Who are Wendy and Bruce?"

"Wendy is the waitress at the counter and Bruce is the cook. They own the place."

"Oh okay. Thank you."

As she ate her breakfast, she filled out the application. When Selma brought it over to Wendy, she looked it over and handed it to Bruce. Danielle watched as the three of them had some discussion and looked over at her a few times. Wendy walked over to Danielle's table.

"So, you want a job here?"

"Yes ma'am. If you will give me one."

"When can you start?"

"Immediately."

"Here then."

Wendy handed her an apron and an order pad.

"Thank you."

Danielle quickly adapted to her new job. She put in a full 8- hrs shift and returned exhausted to the motel room. Before she turned in for the night, she asked the desk clerk for extended stay rates and she paid for the next month.

She didn't know how long after that she would stay, but for now, she was content to stay and save up more money. It was a small town, and she felt safe. That was all that mattered to her at the moment.

Lena and Steven were frantic about Danielle's disappearance. They were relieved when she had finally called them, but her mysteriousness of not telling them where she was worried them. First thing in the morning, they paid a visit to Sergeant Rollins.

"There is nothing we can do. She has left of her own free will and she is an adult. We can't force her to tell you where she is."

This was not what Lena and Steven wanted to hear. They were determined to find their daughter, even if she didn't want to be found. It would be up to them to do what they could to get their daughter back home safely where they felt she belonged. After a few phone calls, they set up an appointment with a prominent private investigator who specialized in tracking down missing persons.

It didn't take them long to get to Mr. Davis's office.

"Mr. and Mrs. Weston, come in and have a seat. I know this must be a difficult time for all of you."

"Thank you, Mr. Davis. Please call me Steven. We just want to find our daughter and get her the help she obviously needs. She has been through so much."

"Yes, of course. First of all, is her cell phone, car, car insurance, any of that in your name?"

"No, none of it is in our name. We tried to foster responsibility and self-sufficiency, so once she was eighteen, we had her get a job and put those things in her own name."

"Okay, so that makes things a bit harder. Not impossible, but harder. If any of those things were in your name, we would have a few options."

"Like what?"

"We could have reported the car stolen if it was in your name. That would have enabled us to put an all-points bulletin out on the car."

"Oh."

"Do you have any of the tracking apps on her phone?"

"She turned off the location sharing."

"Hmm, she definitely does not want you to know where she is. Do you know what prompted this disappearance? Has she done this in the past?"

Lena broke down as she wrung her hands.

"She has never done this before. If something was bothering her in the past, she would come to me or her father to talk through it. The last six months have been crazy, though. I am sure you have seen the news about the Gardiner family. She was best friends with Richard Jr., and was engaged to marry him until she called off the engagement after his siblings died."

"Oh wow. Yes, I am familiar with the saga of the Gardiner family. Tragic. All of it. I imagine she is suffering from a lot of emotional trauma herself. You said she had a job. Where was that?"

"She worked at the café in East Hampton. We didn't know she quit the day after Richard died. She didn't tell us. We went there first when she didn't come home after the funeral. We figured she had picked up a shift to take her mind off everything. That was when they told us she had quit days prior."

"Okay. So she knew she was leaving. I will do what I can to track her down, but there isn't much to go on so far. I will keep you updated as I find anything."

"Thank you."

When they left the private investigator's office, they felt defeated. They had very little hope they would find Danielle. They had to try, though. She was their firstborn, and they didn't want to lose her. They had already endured so much loss recently.

They went home and explained everything to their other two daughters. Neither of them had any idea where their sister had gone and were just as worried and confused as their parents.

CHAPTER TWENTY

Lady Beatrice

THE ATTENTION FROM EVERYONE on the island sent thrilling jolts of excitement through Betty. What she had imagined she would feel didn't even compare to the actual emotions running rampant in her. She had got to her old bungalow before the men of the island came to help her move her stuff. It was imperative that she hide the listening devices and equipment she had used to spy on the family. So she carefully placed it all in the root cellar portion of the basement. Moving an antique armoire in front of the narrow doorway to block anyone from noticing the door. With minutes to spare before the men showed up she finished the task at hand.

Since she was leaving all of her old furniture, it wasn't suspicious that the piece of furniture was being left in the basement either. By late afternoon, all of her personal possessions were moved into Ms. Mary's old room. Looking in the full-length mirror, she pulled her shoulders back and lifted her chin, an air of power radiated from her reflection. The new lady of the manor wanted to throw herself a party to introduce herself to the Hamptons social scene. She went down to the kitchen.

"Stella, I am planning a big soiree. I am going to need to go over the menu with you."

"Sure thing, Betty. When are you planning on having this party?"

"I already asked you once to call me Beatrice. Actually, I prefer Lady Beatrice. I am your employer now, Stella. You must address me accordingly."

Betty had always been a mild-mannered woman. Quietly going about her job. This change in Betty's demeanor took Stella aback. She hadn't expected the change in her status to go so quickly to her head and bring out so much ego. However, it was apparent it already had.

"Yes, ma'am. I apologize for offending you. It won't happen again."

"Make sure it doesn't or I may need to re-evaluate your employment here. I am already skeptical of having you here, considering your son is awaiting trial for murdering my kin."

"Lady Beatrice, surely you are not threatening to fire me because of the allegations against my son? He is innocent until proven guilty in a court of law. And I fully believe in his innocence. I would think you would too, considering you have watched him grow up here."

"I am not the threatening type Stella, I am just telling you how it is. If I feel anyone is a danger to my safety in any way, I will take the necessary precautions. And I am planning the party to occur in two weeks. You will be able to accomplish that, correct?"

"Yes, ma'am."

Stella stood in utter dismay. It was as if this was a different person than the Betty she had worked alongside for many years. Someone she once considered a friend. How could she have changed so drastically in such a short amount of time?

That night when she walked in the door of her home, for the first time in her life, she thought about moving. Her husband John saw the look of frustration and confusion in the worry lines on his wife's face as he took the meals she had prepared for them out of her hands.

"Stella, what has gotten you so worried?"

"Betty, or should I say, Lady Beatrice, as she wants to be called. I had a very uncomfortable interaction with her today. She believes Jimmy is guilty, and she basically threatened to fire me because he is my son."

"Ah, yes, I too had an interesting interaction with her while helping her move. She insisted that we also all call her Lady Beatrice. The security guys told me she has also ordered all the security cameras to be removed from the manor house."

"That makes little sense. Why would she down-grade the security? Jimmy is innocent. He isn't the killer. She is just putting herself in danger."

"We all tried telling her the same thing. Something has her convinced of Jimmy's guilt. And she wants to throw a big party introducing herself to the Hampton socialites as Lady Beatrice in two weeks! It is a logistical nightmare considering we are down four security members. I may have to come out of retirement. There has been an influx of trespassers since the news of the killings broke."

"Do what you have to, John, but if I start feeling we are not welcome here, I may want to consider leaving the island. For good."

"Dear, if you want to leave, we will. I am going to visit Jimmy tomorrow. I will discuss it with him, too."

"John, do you think Betty could have killed everyone and framed Jimmy?"

"You know, before today, I would have said no way. Now, after seeing such a change in her personality, I am not so sure. No one knows how her birth certificate appeared. The more I think about it all, the more suspicious it is."

"Maybe you should discuss all this with Matt? I know he doesn't live on the island anymore, but I am sure he could help sort some of this out."

"You have a point there. I am gonna go call him."

As John left the room, he stopped to hug his wife and give her a peck on the cheek. Her husband's arms wrapped around her gave her comfort in what seemed like a never-ending nightmare.

In his den, John sat in his recliner and dialed his friend Matt.

"Hey there John, how are things going? Sorry to hear about Jimmy's troubles. Just so you know, we don't believe he is the killer. Melissa and I are still doing our own investigating from here."

"Hey Matt, that is so good to hear. We can't seem to make sense of it all. And now, with Betty being named a Gardiner heir and the changes in her personality, it's got Stella and me wondering if she could be the actual killer."

"What did you just say? Betty is a Gardiner?"

"Yup, someone anonymously mailed her birth certificate to Arthur. She seemed just as shocked as everyone else at first, but now she has really slid right into the role of Lady of the Manor House. She is even insisting on being called Lady Beatrice."

"Holy crap! That's crazy. How is she a Gardiner, though?"

"Well, apparently, Alexandria's father had an affair of sorts with her mother, but since she was always so promiscuous, it was an easy secret to keep."

"Oh wow, I remember her mother. I remember our mothers telling us to stay away from her."

"Yeah, I remember that warning, too. Whatever happened to her mother?"

"Didn't she die of a drug or alcohol overdose?"

"Wait, I believe you are correct. In the bungalow, they found her in the bathtub! We should still have those records on file. I am going to pull that file tomorrow."

"She overdosed in the bathtub? I didn't remember that. That is interesting though. I would love to compare the scene of her death with that of Ms. Mary's."

"I will send you a copy of the report by fax tomorrow if I find it. If we find similarities, it might just cast enough doubt on the killer being Jimmy to get him set free. And if there are enough commonalities, it just might shed light on whether Betty could be the actual killer."

"Sounds like a plan. I know Melissa is planning on visiting Jimmy. She wants him to know we are on his side still and we believe in him."

"I am sure he will appreciate that, Matt. Thank you both for all your help."

"No problem. We want to know who the killer is, too. We want justice for Zach and all the others."

"We will get it."

The two friends hung up. John couldn't wait until morning to head to the security shack. He knew he wouldn't get any sleep until he had that file in his hands. So he headed on down to check things out. It took a couple of hours to go through several file cabinets to find the file on Betty's mom's death.

At the time, it was an open and shut case. Everyone knew that she drank and did drugs, so there was no question of her overdosing in the bathtub. He pulled Ms. Mary's report as well. As he read through the reports, glaring similarities jumped out at him. The chair with the bottle of wine and the wineglass. The bottle of pills. All very theatrical. Obviously, the bathrooms were different, but it was eerily ironic. The pictures of the chair with the wine bottle, glass, and pills appeared they could have been from the same crime scene.

As he was sitting at Jimmy's desk going over the files, Samuel walked in, looking concerned.

"Hey, John. I didn't know who to go to, but I saw the lights on in here, so I figured I would come to see who it was. I am glad it's you. At Betty's bungalow, I found something."

"What did you find?"

"Well, I was in the basement, shutting off the water and prepping it to be closed up. Putting sheets over furniture and such. There is an armoire in the basement. I went to put a sheet over and noticed someone had moved it. There were scuff marks on the dirt floor as if they dragged it over several feet. It got me wondering why Betty would have done that by herself. It's a sizeable piece of furniture. So I moved it back."

"And?"

"I found a door to a root cellar behind it."

"What is so mysterious about that?"

"I found many electronic listening devices and boxes of recordings. I listened to some. She had recordings of every conversation that was had in the Manor House. She must have had the whole place bugged."

"Why would Betty be listening in on the family?"

"I don't know, but she would know when and where they were coming and going."

"Where are all the equipment and the recordings now?"

"They are in the back of my truck. I pushed the armoire back to cover the door to make it look as though no one had been in there. But I put everything in my truck and brought it here."

"Great job. Let's put it in here until I can turn it over to the police in the morning. Thank you,

Samuel. I appreciate your help in trying to clear Jimmy's name."

"No problem. He is a good kid, and he didn't do all this. He shouldn't pay for crimes he didn't commit."

"I agree. We need to be careful, though. If Betty is the killer, she is dangerous. She has been doing this for years."

"What do you mean, years?"

"Her mother died similarly as Ms. Mary did."

"You don't think she killed her own mother, do you?"

"I don't know what to think right now. All I know is my son is in jail for crimes he didn't commit and now Lady Beatrice is showing us all a different side of herself."

"Yeah, I can't get used to calling her Lady Beatrice. She will always be Betty to me."

"Same here. She threatened to fire Stella today."

"You are kidding me? Stella is the kindest, most hardworking employee on this island. Why would she fire her?"

"Because she is Jimmy's mother, and she called her Betty."

"Unbelievable."

"Watch your back, Samuel. We do not know what she is capable of."

"I will, and you watch yours and Stella's. If I see or hear anything else, I will let you know."

"Thank you."

CHAPTER TWENTY-ONE

Visitors

JIMMY HAD GOTTEN A new cellmate the day before. The guy snored on the bed beneath him. He was a big burly guy covered in tattoos. He was glad the guy was on the bottom bunk just because of the sheer size of him. Sleep eluded Jimmy already he couldn't imagine trying to sleep on the lower bunk underneath his cellmate. In an effort to lull his mind to sleep he started counting the holes in the ceiling tiles.

His counting was interrupted constantly. The noise of the other inmates yelling at the correction officers, who made their rounds every fifteen minutes. Or by the catcalls made to the female medical personnel who made their rounds twice a day. The amount of respect given to the members of the clergy when they toured always surprised him, though. It got a little quieter during those moments.

Most of the inmates acted like caged animals, pacing in their cells. There had been a fight in the yard the day before, and the prison had been on lockdown for the rest of the day. With the lockdown lifted, Jimmy could feel the tension in the air, as if chaos could ensue at any moment.

Fear caused him to perspire more than usual, with beads of sweat forming on his forehead. He had never been scared for his life before, not even with the serial killer on the island, but now he did not know how to survive in this environment. His stomach tensed and tightened.

His job was security on the island, but he never dealt with hardened criminals before. The inmates were hardcore. Not petty trespassers or vandals. They were murderers and rapists. Being out of his element did not sit well with him.

The realization hit him: he might wind up living in prison for the rest of his life. His stomach churned at the thought. He swallowed hard to hold back from letting his stomach win the battle. Jimmy knew he couldn't survive living here. He missed the island and everything about it. His mother and father, the security crew, everything. The thoughts ran through his head about his cousins and how much he missed them already. How could he let this happen? They were dead because he couldn't protect them. Maybe he was guilty in that sense. But he didn't pull the trigger.

"Jimmy Driscoll, you have a visitor."

The guard's announcement roused Jimmy out of his thoughts. He didn't have a meeting scheduled with his attorney until the next day. Could it be Samuel, again? As the guard led him to the visitor area, it shocked him to see Melissa sitting on the other side of the plexiglass this time.

She was a sight for very sore eyes. Her smile made his heart beat a little faster. The compassion and empathy he saw in her eyes calmed his spirit.

He picked up the phone as she picked up the other one.

"What are you doing here?"

"Checking on you? I wanted to make sure you are okay."

"I am doing as well as expected."

"You look like hell Jimmy."

"I'm not getting sleep. It is noisy as hell in here, never mind the intense fear I have, Melissa. I can't survive in here."

"We are going to get you out of here. Please don't worry."

"How? There is so much circumstantial evidence against me I even sometimes question if I really am guilty."

"Don't say that Jimmy. You know, and I know you didn't kill anyone."

"Okay, but the longer I stay in here, the harder it is for me to have any hope."

"Just hang on, please. Your dad called my dad last night. There might be evidence to clear you."

"What? Samuel called your dad. What evidence?"

"Wait, Samuel? Why do you think Samuel called my dad? I said your dad called my dad. You know, John Driscoll. This place is really getting to you, isn't it? Your dad and my dad were talking because now that Betty is living in the Manor house, she has changed drastically. She is demanding to be called Lady Beatrice. She even threatened to fire your mom. Then they both remembered her mother dying very much like Ms. Mary."

"Okay. Things are getting really confusing. So I need to tell you a secret. Samuel is really Benjamin, who is my biological father. He had no clue he was a Gardiner. He came and visited me when he found out I was a Gardiner and, subsequently, he is too. I am the only one who knows his secret. We suspected him to be the killer originally, but we had eyes on him the entire time of the wedding. So he couldn't have planted the evidence in my bedroom or flown the drone. And he wants to help get me out of here. So now why did Betty threaten to fire my mom? And what is this about Betty's mom dying like Ms. Mary?"

"WOW, that's a lot to unpack! Betty threatened to fire your mom because she called her Betty instead of Lady Beatrice and because she believes you are the killer. Our dads are comparing the files of Betty's mom's death and Ms. Mary's. Apparently, they are eerily alike. And Samuel found tapes of recordings Betty had made of conversations in the Manor house. She had many types of recording equipment and listening devices hidden in a root cellar of her bungalow."

"That's great, but it's all circumstantial evidence. None of it can link her to any of the murders. We need strong direct evidence to clear me and convict her. Right now, there is more circumstantial evidence pointing to me than her."

"Well, they turned everything over to Rolly and your lawyer. Everyone is doing everything they can."

"I appreciate it. It really is great seeing you, Melissa. And it helps to know you are still in my corner."

"Of course, Jimmy, I will always be in your corner. I love you, and when all this is done and over with, maybe we can give ourselves another chance."

"I would love that."

The guard escorted Jimmy back to his cell. His cellmate was awake and grunted at him, so Jimmy just went back to lying on his bed and counting holes again. He finally dozed off, thinking of freedom and his potential future with Melissa. It was late afternoon when the guard awakened him again, telling him he had another visitor. His cellmate piped up.

"Look at you, such a social butterfly. Two visitors in one day, most of us in here barely get a visit a week. You must be the big man on campus."

Jimmy just looked at him and shrugged. It was the guard that responded.

"I would be careful Maddog, this guy is in here for several counts of murder. He is a serial killer. You are in here for attempted murder."

Jimmy watched as his cellmate's eyes widened at the words the guard was saying. He nodded his head toward Jimmy.

"Is that true?"

Jimmy shrugged again.

"That's what they say."

The guard guided Jimmy back to the visitor area. This time, it was his adoptive dad. It was so good to see him. Although Jimmy could see the worry in his eyes. The creases in his forehead were deeper, and the crow's feet around his eyes seemed more prominent.

They both picked up their phones to talk to each other. Jimmy's dad broke down in tears.

"I am sorry son, we are doing everything to get you out of here."

"I know, Dad. It's okay. Melissa stopped by. She filled me in."

"She did? That's great. I am glad to see she is coming back around. I hope when all this mess is clear, you two can start to have a normal relationship again."

"Me too, Dad. Me too. How is Mom? I am worried about her working for Betty. It seems Betty isn't fond of Mom."

"She will be fine, son. If things get too bad, we have already decided we will leave the island."

"You promise me?"

"I promise. We are going to do everything possible to stay safe and get you free so we can all be happy again."

"Okay, give Mom a hug and kiss for me."

"I will."

Their visit was brief, but it was another morale boost for Jimmy. As he got back to his cell, he was feeling more hopeful than he had felt earlier. Until the guard closed the door behind him and walked away. Then his cellmate grabbed him by the collar and jacked him up against the wall.

"You think you are some badass because you murdered a few people?"

"No sir."

"Good, because I can and will kill you if you so much as look at me the wrong way."

"Okay, just put me down and I will give you your space and you can give me mine."

Maddog lowered him back down and Jimmy climbed back into his bunk and resumed counting the holes in the ceiling tiles. It was another restless night. There was banging on the bars and yelling again, and Maddog snoring. He tried to drown out the noise with his pillow as he closed his eyes and thought about Melissa again.

Jimmy imagined it was early in the morning when things finally quieted down and he could fall asleep. It felt good to get some sleep. He woke up choking on smoke and panicked. Jumping from his bed, he yelled for the guards. His heart was beating fast as he realized the fire was in his cell, and his cellmate just sat and laughed.

The guards got there to the cell and put out the small fire with an extinguisher. Maddog blamed Jimmy for starting the fire and they moved Jimmy to segregation housing.

For the rest of the day, Jimmy tried to just sleep. His cellmate in segregation housing was quieter, which was a plus. He knew he didn't start the fire, and he remembered Maddog's threats. Why would this guy start a fire and get him moved? What beef does this guy have? He must have looked at him the wrong way.

Prison life was already wearing thin on Jimmy's nerves. He just wanted out, but couldn't figure out how he was going to get out of this mess.

CHAPTER TWENTY-TWO

New Boss

LADY BEATRICE WAS ACCOMPANYING Arthur into the city for her first board meeting. She was determined to make sure everyone knew she was in charge. Her appearance was much different now. She had burned the old grey maid uniform she wore in the past the first day she moved into the Manor house. The power suit, skirt, and blouse she wore now with three-inch heels exuded confidence and power.

As they rode the train, she took in the eyes, watching her. They only made her sit up straighter, with her shoulders back and her chin up slightly higher. She wanted everyone to know she was important.

When they reached the office building that she was now in charge of, excitement ran through her veins. Power. This was everything she had worked so hard for.

People shook her hand and welcomed her as they made their way through the building and up to the boardroom. She shook hands back, although looked down upon everyone she came in contact with. When anyone called her Betty, she sharply corrected them to call her Lady Beatrice.

She took her position at the head of the conference table as Arthur introduced her to the board members.

"This is Lady Beatrice. She is now the new co-owner of Cromwell Realtor Corporation and Gardiners Island. Please make her feel welcome."

After each board member went around the room and welcomed her and introduced themselves, Lady Beatrice addressed them all.

"Thank you for the warm welcome. As Arthur has mentioned, I am in charge now. I will finalize all decisions. I will listen to everyone's input and weigh opinions, but in the end, the only opinion that really matters is mine. Does everyone understand?"

Arthur's mouth dropped open and everyone else's around the room did, too. Allison looked at Arthur as Arthur responded.

"Lady Beatrice, with all due respect. All of us have been running this business for years. I would hope that you rethink your position and your statement."

"Arthur, I am in charge here. Not you. I can fire and replace all of you if you don't agree with what I stated."

They exchanged looks among all the board members. Eyebrows raised and heads bowed with pursed lips. Bodies shifted awkwardly in chairs and tension filled the room. No one felt comfortable with how this meeting was starting off, except Lady Beatrice herself. Allison broke the silence.

"Well then, I guess we should all bring you up to speed on what is happening within the company then, so you can make informed decisions."

"Thank you, Allison. That is appreciated. Oh, and I am sorry for the loss of your son- and daughter-in-law. Such a tragedy."

"Thank you, Lady Beatrice. And yes, it was a tragedy. It was a deep blow to all of us personally and to the business. Jessica was a tremendous asset to this company. She is missed dearly."

Allison's words cut through Lady Beatrice. The smug smile that had been on Lady Beatrice's face since entering the boardroom thinned into a neutral, resting scowl. Allison knew the shot she fired across the bow had hit its mark, and she smiled sweetly back at Lady Beatrice. She didn't care if she got fired. Arthur already knew her plans.

Allison had control of the property in Ireland that Jessica and Timothy had purchased. She was planning on moving there in six months. So if she got fired by Lady Beatrice, she really didn't care. She hadn't worked her entire life at this company to let some power-hungry control freak tell her what to do.

Lady Beatrice kept her composure, however, she was fuming inside. She did not like the idolization of Jessica. It made her blood boil. She regretted not taking Allison out of the equation when she had the chance at the wedding.

Each board member gave a detailed report on the various projects they were in charge of. Lady Beatrice gave her unsolicited and uninformed opinions about each. Many times over making poor business decisions that would cost the company money. She overrode any votes and claimed she had the final say in all matters.

When the meeting was over, Arthur accompanied Lady Beatrice back to the Manor house, where they would be interviewing candidates for several new security positions and the new housekeeper. Martin had been pulling double duty since Lady Beatrice had moved into the Manor house. He ushered each potential candidate into the parlor when it was time for them to be interviewed.

They filled the security positions first, and Arthur felt confident about each one Lady Beatrice had hired. He was thankful he had pre-screened the applicants beforehand without her knowledge, so that those without the proper qualities needed for the job were weeded out.

When it came time to interview the housekeeper candidates, it was between three potential employees. Arthur knew which one he wanted to hire, but ultimately, the decision would be Lady Beatrice's. He hoped to come up with a way to persuade her to pick the one he favored without her catching on that he favored her.

The first potential employee was a young woman named Mindi. She was just 18 and had no prior work experience. Lady Beatrice eyed her up and down as she walked into the room and sat down across from her.

"So, why do you want to work for me?"

The straightforward question and the briskness in the tone in which Lady Beatrice asked it threw off Mindi.

"Um, well. Ma'am, everybody who is anybody around here is curious about this place. You know, so I need a job and figured why not? At least it wouldn't be boring, right?"

Lady Beatrice frowned. She didn't like this one. This one seemed a bit too eager and curious. What she didn't need was a snooping employee.

"I see. You do know curiosity killed the cat, don't you?"

Mindi's eyes widened at Lady Beatrice's reply. There were a few more questions and answers between the two, and then she was dismissed without getting the position.

The next one was a little older. She was 22 and her name was Lorraine. She had previously worked as a nanny and a housekeeper for one of the prominent families of East Hampton.

"I see you worked for the Hammervilles. Why did you leave their employment?"

"Well, to be completely honest. Mr. Hammerville was a bit inappropriate towards me, and it felt extremely uncomfortable. So I quit. I have been waitressing until I can find something better."

Lady Beatrice took pleasure in the revealed secret of the prominent family. She loved collecting secrets about people. They could always be used to her advantage. It is a shame this girl didn't share her passion for power. The poor girl didn't even realize the missed opportunity she had.

"Oh, what a shame. That must have been such a horrible experience for you."

After more questions and answers back and forth and again, Lady Beatrice dismissed Lorraine without hiring her.

The last candidate was a 32-year-old with over twelve years of experience as a housekeeper for one of the elderly gentlemen in East Hampton who had just passed away, leaving her jobless. Her name was Verna.

"Well, Verna, you are our last hope. I see you have experience and you present yourself maturely, unlike the other candidates for this position. Tell me, why should I hire you?"

"Lady Beatrice, as you know, I have worked for a very prominent family in the past. I know how to keep confidential information and I know how to do my job while staying out of family matters. You will barely notice I am here unless I am performing a task that you require to be done in the presence of others."

Lady Beatrice smiled and nodded at Arthur. Arthur was relieved she picked the candidate he wanted her to.

"Arthur, I believe we have found our new house-keeper. Please have Martin show her to her new home and have him show her the duties she is responsible for performing."

Arthur ushered Verna out of the parlor and intro-duced her to Martin. Martin took over in showing Verna the Manor house and her responsibilities. When he was done, he showed her to the bun-galow Betty had once lived in, which would now be her home. Samuel came by to make sure he turned all the utilities back on and that they were in working order.

Verna unpacked her things, changed into her crisp new uniform, and headed back to the Manor house to get to work. It was after dinner and she knew she had to draw a bath for Lady Beatrice and turn down her bedspread.

When she reached the door of Lady Beatrice, she knocked on the door.

"Come on in."

Lady Beatrice was sitting at her desk writing in what looked like a diary or journal of some sort. When she saw Verna, she closed the book, slid it into the desk drawer, and locked it closed. She held onto the key and slipped it into her bathrobe pocket. Verna watched all of this carefully.

"I am here to run your bath water and turn down your bedspread."

"Then get to it, please. At least you are punctual. You don't have to tell me why you are here, though. I already know. Please, just do your work."

Verna went into the bathroom and started the bath water. She wondered how she would get access to the desk drawer. It would be imperative that she read what Lady Beatrice wrote in the diary. When the bath was full, she went back into the bedroom and turned down the bedspread as Lady

Beatrice entered the bathroom and shut the door behind her.

With a slim glimmer of hope that the lock on the desk drawer didn't actually work, Verna tried opening it. It disappointed her when it didn't budge. She needed to figure out how to get that diary, but tonight would not be the time.

She finished the rest of her nightly tasks that were required of her and then headed back to the bungalow. As she looked around at the dingy and dusty place, it boggled her mind that the former housekeeper lived there. It definitely wasn't the definition of clean, but then again, she had known carpenters who had unfinished projects at their own houses. She spent the rest of the evening scrubbing and cleaning the small bungalow.

In the bedroom's closet, it surprised Verna to find an old high school yearbook. She thumbed through it. Finding that it had belonged to Lady Beatrice. There was no one who had signed it. No teachers. No friends. Nobody. There were faces crossed out. Devil horns added to some. There weren't many pictures of the young Betty. However, she was interestingly in drama club. This was an excellent find. Verna would keep it. It would be an early morning the next day, so she turned in to get some sleep.

Lady Beatrice finished her bath and then sat down at her desk. She unlocked the drawer and took out the diary. She completed her daily entry. Since she was a child, she had been writing in it. The desk drawer held several journals already filled with her daily life. It was imperative that nobody get ahold of them, which is why she guarded them under lock and key. The key went with her everywhere she went. It was never out of her possession.

She knew the secrets revealed between those pages could be her demise. So she would do everything she could to keep that from happening. If she burned them, it would ensure that no one would use them against her. However, she wanted them to be read, eventually. When she died, she wanted people to know how powerful she had been. They were her last legacy.

CHAPTER TWENTY-THREE

Starting Over

DANIELLE HAD BEEN LIVING out of the motel room for two weeks now. She went to work daily at the diner. They loved her there. The customers loved her charm and her attention to detail when serving them. She was efficient. It was her first day off since she had started.

The first order of business was she needed to find a more permanent place to live. She had decided to settle down in this small town. An efficiency apartment would be perfect if she could find one. She opened up the classified page of the local newspaper and started her search. Going through the columns, she found three that looked promising, so she circled them.

She set up appointments for the afternoon to check them out. Her phone rang, and she looked at the screen. It was her mom, again. She called daily, leaving her a message begging her to come home. This time, she picked up.

"Hi, mom."

"Oh Danielle, it's so good to hear your voice. Your texts are always so short and monotonous."

"Well, mom. Like I keep saying in my texts, I am fine. I am safe."

"That's good honey. But we miss you. Why can't you tell us where you are? Why can't we come to see you?"

"It's better for everyone if I don't tell you where I am or why you can't see me. Tell me what you have been up to?"

"I am worried about you. That's what I am up to. Your father misses you. Your sisters miss you. You have turned our lives upside down."

"I am sorry mom, You will understand eventually. Any fresh news there? Anything on Jimmy?"

"Jimmy is still in jail, thank god. I can't believe he killed his own family members. But I guess greed does that to people. The joke is on him, though. He isn't the only heir to the Gardiner fortune."

"What? First of all, if you believe Jimmy killed them, you obviously do not know him. He considered his cousins more like siblings he never had. And who is this heir you are talking about?"

"Well, it appears Betty the housekeeper was a product of an affair. She is Ms. Alexandria's half-sister. Although, she calls herself Lady Beatrice now. She is having a big party tomorrow night at the Manor house, introducing herself to society. They have invited all the elite socialites. Anyone who is anyone is going."

"Oh, my god. You are kidding me. Betty? A Gardiner? Are you and Dad going to this party?"

"Of course we are going!"

"Mom, please be careful."

"Why? The killer is behind bars. I know you don't believe Jimmy did it, but the police arrested him. They don't arrest innocent people."

"Mom, it happens all the time. Please just be careful, that's all I ask."

"Danielle, all I ask is that you tell us where you are."

"That's not possible, mom. I love you. I gotta go."

"Love you too."

The news that Betty was a Gardiner and was now living the high life in the Manor house as Lady Beatrice left Danielle more than just a little unsettled. It solidified her belief she did the right thing in getting away and not telling anyone where she was going or why. It also strengthened her conviction that Jimmy was innocent.

She wished her parents would stay far away from the island and the Manor house. Unfortunately, though, she knew her parents and grandmother were so entrenched in the Hampton social scene. She prayed they all stayed safe.

Danielle took a shower and then headed out to look at the three apartments. The first one was really a small one-bedroom house on the property of a bigger house. It was cute, with an eat-in kitchen and a small living room. The bathroom was a decent size. The bedroom was too small, though. Danielle had to think about when the baby was born. She needed room for a crib.

The second apartment was a loft above a garage converted into a one-bedroom apartment. The size was substantial, but the stairs concerned Danielle with the thought of carrying the baby up and down them constantly.

The third one was the one that captured her heart. It was a cottage with a small stream bordering the yard. It had two small bedrooms, a bathroom, an eat-in kitchen, and a living room. The owner was an older woman, named Ms. Ditters, who lived next door in an old Victorian-type house. She explained the cottage had once served as the servant's quarters.

Danielle felt at home.

"What is the rent again?"

"I usually ask $1000 a month, but I have a good feeling about you. I want to give you a deal. $800 a month. First and last month up front."

"I will take it! Thank you! Can I move in, in two weeks? I have already paid for the motel ahead of time that I am staying in."

"Absolutely! You can move in when you want to."

"Thank you! Oh, I think I should tell you since you are my new landlord. I will be having a baby in about six months. I hope it's still okay if I rent from you?"

"I already knew, dear."

The old woman smiled at Danielle. It startled her. She didn't think her baby bump was showing yet.

"How did you know?"

"You are glowing, us old timers can tell."

Danielle smiled and thanked the woman again. She felt like this was going to be the perfect place for her and her child to start their new life. Then she realized she needed to find herself an obstetrician. That was the next item on her agenda for the day. She called around and finally got in for an appointment in the next week.

She was tired by the end of the day. When her head hit the pillow and she closed her eyes instead of seeing Richard lying in a pool of his own blood or in his casket, she saw the cottage and her holding her child, cradling them in her arms.

For the first time in weeks, she didn't cry herself to sleep. She peacefully drifted into a restful slumber. She woke up the next morning more refreshed than she had felt in a long time. When she got to work, even Wendy quipped at how chipper she looked.

"Good morning, Danielle. You look like a ray of sunshine this morning. That day off did wonders for you. I am sorry we have been working you so hard. We hired another waitress to lighten the load, too."

"Thanks, Wendy. I guess I didn't realize how much a good night's sleep can do for the soul until I finally got one."

"Well, those dark circles are fading. Hopefully, a couple more good nights and they will be gone for you."

"I didn't realize my fatigue showed so much."

"Dear, people round here notice more than most folks. Oh, and your new landlord stopped in last night. Old Doc Ditters. I am glad you found a permanent home. I was worried you would leave us when your time was up at the motel."

"Doc Ditters?"

"Yeah, Old Doc Ditters, she is the oldest obstetrician in the area still practicing. She runs the Family Obstetrics practice on Hollow Road."

Danielle laughed to herself.

"That all makes sense now."

"What makes sense?"

"How she knew before I told her."

"How she knew what before you told her what?"

"Oh, I am sorry Wendy. I should have told you sooner, too. I hope it doesn't affect my work here. The baby is due in six months. I am pregnant. On my next day off, I will have an appointment with Doc Ditters."

"Not much gets past Doc Ditters. And yes, it's okay you didn't tell me. You are telling me now. You are one of the best waitresses we have ever had. We aren't going to lose you."

Danielle got to work filling the salt and pepper shakers and the sugar containers on all the tables as the morning regulars started filing in. Wendy came out with an old mayonnaise jar cleaned out and a piece of paper stuck to it. She placed it next to the cash register. Danielle was curious about what it was for. It wasn't uncommon for restaurants to raise funds for various charities. She wanted to know what one they were raising money for.

"Hey Wendy, what is that for?"

"You, my dear! It's the Danielle maternity leave fund! We have six months to fill this jar to help you out!"

"Are you serious? Thank you so much!"

"Who's having a baby?"

Pete, the regular who had just sat down, piped up.

"I am."

Danielle answered as she filled his coffee cup and plated a blueberry muffin without him even asking.

"Who is the lucky father?"

Pete broke a piece of muffin off and popped it into his mouth.

Danielle swallowed the lump in her throat and fought back the tears.

"He is dead, unfortunately."

"I am so sorry."

Pete reached across the counter and squeezed Danielle's hand.

"Thanks."

Danielle became occupied with other customers and settled into her day. She didn't notice the hundred-dollar bill Pete had slipped into her maternity leave fund. Wendy did, and she smiled to herself.

CHAPTER TWENTY-FOUR

The Big Soiree

I T WAS THE NIGHT of Lady Beatrice's big soiree. Stella had been cooking all day since Lady Beatrice refused to have it catered. Verna did what she could do to help, however, her workload had been doubled as well. John was in the kitchen dressed as a server, as most of the inhabitants of the island were as well. Lady Beatrice invited none of them to the big party as guests.

Verna had tried every chance she could to get into the locked desk drawer. On one or two occasions, Lady Beatrice almost caught her in the act. Not knowing what she wrote in the diary consumed Verna's thoughts, day and night. She was certain whatever was written in it was very important since Lady Beatrice kept it so guarded.

As guests filed into the Manor house, Lady Beatrice stood inside the entrance and welcomed them personally. Her attire was regal in her mind. She had chosen a purple spaghetti strap dress with a scoop neckline. It gave the appearance of curves where she had none. The hairdresser she had hired pinned her hair in an updo, and she had a small tiara placed strategically on her hair. Arthur did the introductions since this was the first time most of the socialites were being introduced to Lady Beatrice.

When her introductions to Mr. and Mrs. Hammerville occurred, she noted how good-looking Mr. Hammerville was. It was good to have secret knowledge of him. She would definitely use that to her advantage. Rita showed up on the arm of Samuel and Lady Beatrice bristled.

"I did not invite employees as guests to this party, Samuel."

"My invitation included a plus one, and he is my escort."

"Ms. Duvall, I understand that you have different standards than I do, but how would that reflect on all my other employees? If I let him into the party and not the others, that would be me showing favoritism."

"There is a simple solution, Lady Beatrice. I quit as your employee, and now I am just my lovely date's escort. I will remove my things from my quarters tonight."

Samuel escorted Rita right past Lady Beatrice, who clenched and unclenched her fists at her sides. They were the last of the guests to show up, so Lady Beatrice went to the bar to get herself a drink. It pleasantly surprised her to see Mr. Hammerville bellying up to the bar himself.

"I do hope you are enjoying yourself, Mr. Hammerville."

Lady Beatrice slid her hand down his arm as she sidled up next to him at the bar. He downed his shot of whiskey and ordered another.

"You can call me Mike."

"Ah, I like that name. Mike. It's strong. Are you powerful, Mike?"

"Depends on who you ask, I guess."

"I am asking you."

He swallowed the second shot and asked for a third.

"Well, yes, I am powerful. Is that what you like, Lady Beatrice?"

"Yes. Powerful is exactly my type. And you can call me just Beatrice."

Lady Beatrice picked up her drink with one hand, turned while trailing the other down his arm again, and walked away to mingle with the crowd. She was certain she had just planted the right seed. He would seek her out, eventually.

Oh, the gossip that these people spread was tantalizing. She would have so much to write in her diary. Hearing these secrets straight from the people themselves gave her a whole new rush. As she looked over at the bar, she saw Mike and his wife. His wife looked mad, her face was flushed red, and she was grabbing for his drink. He, of course, kept it from her and downed it in one swift gulp. This didn't sit well with his wife. She turned and stormed off. Lady Beatrice thought to herself,

Hmm, trouble in paradise. No wonder he was looking for love with the nanny.

Lady Beatrice felt on top of the world. By the end of the night, exhaustion set in from talking to everyone. As the last of the guests left, she realized there was one still standing at the bar. It was Mike.

"Mike, where is your lovely wife?"

"She left hours ago."

"Oh, she did. Do I need to call you a cab?"

"No, I was thinking I could just spend the night with you."

"Did you, really? And what made you think I would want you to spend the night?"

"Beatrice, we both know you do."

As he finished his sentence, he finished his last drink, took Lady Beatrice's hand, and led her upstairs. At the top of the stairs, he stopped.

"I do not know which room is yours, so you are going to have to lead the way."

Lady Beatrice smiled and led him the rest of the way to her room. As she opened the door, she pulled Mike along with her. She let go of his hand

and slipped out of her dress, letting it fall to the floor. Mike looked her up and down. The smile on his face and the lust in his eyes told her he liked what he saw.

"You are a very mysterious woman, Lady Beatrice. Where have you been hiding away all these years?"

"I have been here all along, waiting in the wings for just the right time."

Lady Beatrice wrapped her arms around Mike's neck and pulled him closer. She brushed her lips against his. He couldn't resist any longer. Lifting her up, he carried her over to the bed. She helped remove his clothes in a flurry of heated passion. This was power. She had craved this her entire life. She had finally fulfilled her destiny.

In the morning, she awoke to an empty bed and a note on the pillow.

Dear Beatrice,

Thank you for a wonderful evening. I look forward to many more.

Love Mike.

She smiled. This was everything she had always wanted. Power, prestige, love interests. Nobody could stop her now. She called down to the kitchen through the new intercom system.

"Stella, could you have Verna bring my breakfast up to me this morning? I feel like having breakfast in bed."

"Yes, ma'am. She will bring it up momentarily."

Verna was upstairs within fifteen minutes, carrying a breakfast tray. She knocked on the door.

"Come in."

She walked in and Lady Beatrice was still in bed.

"Bring it here and put it over my lap."

Verna did as she was told. She watched as Lady Beatrice took a bottle of eye drops and put them in her eyes right over her food tray.

"Lady Beatrice, you know you should be careful with those eye drops. You could poison yourself if it gets in your food and you ingest it."

"Don't be ridiculous Verna, I know how to put eye drops in my eyes. I have been doing it for years. None is going into my food."

As Lady Beatrice ranted with the bottle in her hand, she hadn't noticed several drops had in fact fallen into her breakfast.

"Don't say I didn't warn you."

"You are dismissed. Don't you have work to do?"

"Yes, ma'am."

Verna left the room to finish her morning routine. The woman was batshit crazy. She was going to poison herself if she continued to do that.

Lady Beatrice ate her breakfast and then got out her diary to write in. It wasn't long before she felt sick to her stomach and dizzy. She attempted to call Stella through the intercom to have Verna bring her something to settle her stomach, but Stella wasn't answering. She did not know where in the house Verna or Martin were, so she decided she would attempt to go to the kitchen herself.

She hugged the wall as she made her way to the stairs. The pain in her stomach was getting worse. Her vision was blurring as well. Making it to the stairs, she gripped the railing with both hands to steady herself. Her breathing was becoming laborious. The outer edges of her vision closed in until darkness consumed them. She lost her footing and tumbled down the stairs, coming to an abrupt stop at the bottom, and crashing into a small table holding a vase of flowers.

The noise of Lady Beatrice falling down the stairs and crashing into the table echoed through-out the house. Martin, Verna, and Stella all came running. The sight of Lady Beatrice at the bottom of the stairs caught them all by surprise. Verna was the first to come out of the shock and went to render first aid.

"Stella, call the ambulance! Martin, get me some towels or anything to stop the bleeding!"

Soon, emergency personnel and chaos filled the house. Hours after they had transported her to the hospital, Sergeant Rollins returned with the news that Lady Beatrice had succumbed to her injuries. Stella was the first to break the silence.

"What happened?"

"I was going to ask you three the same question. You were the only ones in the house with her, right?"

It was Verna who spoke up next.

"Serg, we were all outside. I was just coming in from hanging sheets on the line to dry. Stella here was in the kitchen garden cutting herbs, and Martin was bringing the runners in from shaking them out. We all came inside together and heard the crash. We found her at the bottom of the stairs. I have a theory, though."

"What's your theory, Verna?"

"She accidentally poisoned herself with her eye drops."

"How the heck did she do that?"

Verna relayed what had happened earlier when she brought Lady Beatrice her breakfast.

"Thanks, I am going to call the hospital and let them know to test for that. I am also going to have my investigative team come and look over her room and take pictures and prints. To rule out foul play, considering everything that has happened here in the recent past."

"Oh, Serg. You may want your investigators to check out her desk drawer. It's locked, but she keeps her diary in there. I couldn't get in."

"Thanks, Verna."

Stella just watched as Verna and Sergeant Rollins conversed. It filled her with confusion.

"Verna, why do you keep calling Sergeant Rollins, Serg?"

Verna looked at Sergeant Rollins. He nodded his head.

"Stella, I am an undercover detective. We were investigating Lady Beatrice to clear Jimmy. After Samuel found the listening devices in her bungalow, our suspicions grew. We needed more direct evidence, though. They put me here to try to find some."

Stella burst into tears. Martin put his arm around her.

"I am going to bring her home to John unless you two need anything more from us."

"We are good. I will have an officer come and get your official statements as to where you all were at the time of her fall. Seeing as you all were together, I don't see any issues."

The investigative team dusted for prints, took pictures, and picked the lock of the desk drawer. When they started reading through the many journals tucked away in it, they immediately called Sergeant Rollins back to the Manor house.

"Serg, you need to get these to the state prosecutor's office and Jimmy's attorney ASAP. They clear him of any wrongdoing. It's all here, in gruesome detail. She was the serial killer, not Jimmy."

"Good work team. I think it's safe to say this case is closed. Unless you found any evidence of foul play with today's events, I think we can chalk this up to accidental poisoning."

"We found only one set of prints on the bottle of eye drops, Serg. We assume they are hers."

"Okay, follow up on that and make sure the prints match, so we don't get caught up on any loopholes."

"Roger that, Serg,"

Sergeant Rollins left the Manor house and called the prosecutor's office and Jimmy's attorney with the news. When he was done, he sat back in his chair and smiled. It was a great feeling when justice was served. He was happy that his friend would be out of jail soon and back home, where he belonged.

CHAPTER TWENTY-FIVE

Sweet Freedom

A GUARD WOKE JIMMY up.

"Hey, Jimmy Driscoll, it's your lucky day. Grab your belongings. You are being released."

"Are you serious? Or am I dreaming?"

"You're not dreaming. Come on, your lawyer is waiting for you."

Jimmy was dazed and confused as he followed the guard to where his lawyer was waiting for him with his release paperwork.

"Hey, Jimmy, sign right here and you are a free man."

"Okay, what changed? How is all this happening?"

"Well, there have been some startling develop-
ments in the serial murders of the Gardiner family. First, Betty, or Lady Beatrice as she liked to
be called, is dead. Seems she accidentally poisoned herself with her eye drops. Then, when they
were investigating her death, they found count-
less journals detailing the crimes that she committed. There, in her own writing, she confessed
to the murders and framing you."

Jimmy's eyes welled up with the realization he
was a free man again. He hugged his lawyer and
then they walked out of the correctional facility.
As they got in his lawyer's car, Jimmy stopped for
a moment and took in a breath of fresh air.

"I wasn't sure this moment was ever going to
happen. Not that I didn't have faith in you or the
others working to get me out, but while I was in
there, I couldn't see a way out."

"Well, Jimmy, you had many people in your corner. We were determined to get you out. I hope
you are ready for a party because everyone is
waiting for you back at the Manor house."

"I am absolutely ready to party!"

It took them several hours to make it back to the island and walk in the doors of the Manor house. When Jimmy did, the first person he saw was his mom, Stella. He wrapped her in the biggest hug and squeezed her as if he never wanted to let her go again. She reciprocated just as fiercely as the tears flowed down her cheeks freely.

It took several minutes for all the hugs to be exchanged between everyone. Melissa and her parents were there. Allison and Jack were happy to see Jimmy free and were there to celebrate along with Arthur. Even Rolly was there to celebrate.

It overwhelmed Jimmy with happiness that he was free. However, the sadness of the loss of his cousins overshadowed the joy. Melissa could see the anguish of the battling emotions on his face.

"Hey, you want to go for a walk and get a little fresh air?"

"I would love that, thanks."

Jimmy took her hand, and they excused themselves from the party. They wound up walking over to the family cemetery. The feelings of guilt washed over him. He hadn't been able to protect his cousins, especially on their special day. Dropping to his knees in front of their graves, he openly wept. Melissa knelt down beside him and put her arms around his shoulders.

"I am so sorry. I couldn't protect you all."

"Hey, you did your best, and that's all we could ask."

Jimmy's head snapped up as he looked at Melissa and it registered she had heard the voice, too. They both stood up to see Timothy smiling behind them.

"What the hell? We thought you were dead. They had a funeral and all. I couldn't attend, but they had it. They charged me with your murder! Is Jessica alive too? And Richard? Please tell me they are alive, too."

"I am so sorry we had to lie to you. Jessica is alive. Well, she is in a medically induced coma. She is stable. There is a bullet fragment lodged very close to her spine. They can't operate yet. It's too risky for her and the baby. Richard, unfortunately, his wounds were fatal."

"Oh my God! Jessica is pregnant but alive!"

Jimmy ran his fingers through his hair in disbelief.

"Again, we are sorry we had to lie. It was the only way to keep Jessica and the baby safe. To tell everyone we were dead. We knew you weren't the killer. We had to draw the actual killer out. The decision was made between me and Arthur to go ahead with the plan we had discussed before. We knew you were being framed. It was the only way."

Jimmy pulled Timothy into a big bear hug.

"I get it and I forgive you. When can I see Jessica and visit her?"

"Tomorrow we will go see her, but today we celebrate your freedom."

"Do they all know inside?"

"Arthur, Allison, and Rolly know. No one else could know. We had to limit who knew to pull it off."

"Okay, well, let's let everyone else in on the secret then!"

"After you."

Timothy followed Jimmy and Melissa as they headed back into the Manor house.

"Hey everyone, I got another big surprise. Look what the cat dragged in."

Jimmy stepped aside and showed Timothy standing behind him. There were gasps and looks of confusion on the faces of those not in on the secret. Jimmy filled them all in. They were all excited to hear that Jessica was alive too, even though she had a tough battle ahead of her.

The celebration went on until everyone was just too tired to party anymore. Timothy left to go back and stay at the hospital with Jessica, where he had been by her side for weeks. Allison, Arthur, and Jack left to go home. The only person who stayed was Melissa.

"Are you okay staying on the island now?"

"Yes, now that the evil is gone, I will stay on the island with you. If the offer still stands?"

"Of course, it still stands. I have always wanted to marry you, Melissa. I love you."

"I love you too, Jimmy."

The next morning, Stella was in the kitchen making her son breakfast like she normally did. The killer had gotten what she deserved, and she was content that her son was free. She opened the cabinet to get some salt and pepper to season the scrambled eggs she was making. She knew that's how Jimmy liked them. Pausing when she saw the bottle of eye drops.

Who would have guessed the crazy Lady Beatrice would accidentally add more eye drops to her breakfast that morning? Stella had resigned to poison her slowly. She took the bottle and threw it in the trash, covering it with the broken eggshells. No one would know what she had done to save her baby boy from going to prison for the rest of his life.

She washed her hands and finished making breakfast. Jimmy and Melissa came down together, grabbed some plates with eggs and coffee, and sat at the island in the kitchen to eat.

"Thanks for the breakfast, mom. You don't know how much I missed your home cooking."

"You are welcome. You don't know how much I missed cooking for someone who appreciates my cooking."

"Hey, mom, where was Samuel yesterday?"

"Oh, he quit the night of Lady Beatrice's party. I think he moved in with Rita. Why are you so concerned about him, son?"

"I feel like I owe him an apology. We thought he was the killer."

Jimmy hated lying to his mother, but he had promised Samuel he would keep his secret. He would go to Rita's to see him in person and offer him his job back.

"I am going to stop by Rita's and talk to him on my way to go visit Jessica in the hospital."

"Okay, send our love and prayers to Jessica and the baby."

"I will, mom."

Jimmy and Melissa drove to Rita's house and rang the bell. When Rita answered the door, the look on her face was one of puzzlement.

"Hi Rita, is Samuel here?"

"Yes, he is. Why are you out of jail?"

"Oh, I guess the news hasn't hit the papers yet. Lady Beatrice accidentally poisoned herself and during her death investigation, they found journals she had written detailing her crimes, including framing me for all the murders."

"WOW. Nope, hadn't heard that news, but that's wonderful you have been cleared. Come on in and I will get Samuel for you."

Rita ushered them inside her living room and went to tell Samuel they were there to see him. As he came downstairs with Rita, he was smiling.

"Is it true? Did Lady Beatrice confess to the killings and poison herself?"

"Yup, it's all true. I am here to offer you your job back on the island if you want it."

"Can I commute to work?"

"Absolutely! Nothing says you have to live on the island. That's just a perk most people choose to take."

"Then yes, I would love to have my job back. Can I speak to you privately, though, out on the back deck?"

"Sure."

Jimmy followed Samuel onto the back deck.

"You haven't told anyone I am your biological father, have you?"

"Well, I told Melissa. She won't tell anyone. I promise."

"Okay. I trust you both. You know my past, son. I am sorry for my sins and I know someday I will atone for them fully, but I am happy with Rita and my life now. There is no reason for any of it to be brought out. I don't care about the Gardiner fortune. I care about having a relationship with you, though, even if we have to pass it off as a friendship."

"I would also like to have that relationship. Your secret is safe with me. Oh, by the way. Timothy and Jessica are both alive. Well, Jessica is in a medically induced coma and pregnant, but she is alive. We are going to visit her now."

"Well, tell her she is one tough cookie and she can make it through this."

"I will. Thanks for all your help and support."

"Anytime kid, Anytime."

Jimmy and Melissa left Rita's house and headed to the hospital to visit with Jessica. Jimmy was nervous. He didn't know what to expect. They walked into her hospital room and saw Timothy sitting beside her, holding her hand. There were machines beeping, and many things hooked up to her.

"Hey guys, I told Jessica the news. The doctors say she can hear us. She responds by squeezing your hand too."

Jimmy went over and held Jessica's hand.

"Hey cuz. We did it, we found out who the killer was. She's dead. I guess that's justice. It's kind of poetic that she poisoned herself and fell down the stairs."

Jessica squeezed Jimmy's hand, and a tear slid down his cheek.

"Oh, yeah. Samuel said you are one tough cookie, and he knows you are going to get through this."

Jessica squeezed his hand again. Jimmy and Melissa stayed a short time and then headed back to the island and the start of their life together. They had a wedding to plan and some rearranging of furniture again because Jimmy was bringing back the pool table.

Jimmy's phone rang, and it perplexed him that it was Rolly on the other end.

"Hey Jimmy, I hate to bother you. I know you are probably still celebrating your freedom and all. I just have some questions and figured you are the one to ask."

"Sure, Rolly. No problem. What do you need?"

"Well, first, we don't know what to do with Betty's body. Who to turn her over to for burial? Technically, since she has family, we have to ask you all."

"Wow, that isn't something we were even thinking about ourselves. Can I talk to the others about it and get back to you?"

"Sure thing. Then there is another dilemma. Her journals Jimmy. They contain a lot of dirt. On the family and others in the community. Nothing necessarily criminal, but the information in the wrong hands could be used against these people. We photocopied the pages detailing her crimes and her framing you for our records. I am thinking we should turn the journals back over to you and let you guys destroy them."

"Yeah, let me discuss that with the others, too. I will get back to you."

"Okay, Jimmy. Just let me know as soon as possible. By the way, it's great to have you back."

"Thanks, Rolly, for everything."

"No problem."

CHAPTER TWENTY-SIX

New Friendship

DANIELLE HAD MOVED INTO the cottage early even though she couldn't get a refund of the money she had paid upfront to the motel. The cottage was just homey, and she loved living there on her own. Her first appointment with Doc Ditters went well, and she was told the baby was growing according to schedule.

Pete had become more than just a regular customer. He offered to help her move and get items for the baby coming. They even went out to dinner a couple of times. He knew she was still mourning the loss of Richard, so he was willing to just be a supportive friend for now.

She had ignored several of her mother's calls, but one particular morning, her mother would not stop calling. She answered it.

"Yes Mother, I am still okay. I am still safe and no, I will not tell you where I am. Please stop calling me repeatedly."

"Danielle, I am trying to call you because I have important news."

Guilt crept over Danielle. She prayed her father and sisters were okay.

"I am sorry, Mom. What's going on? Is Dad okay? Are Erica and Stephanie okay?"

"Yes, they are all fine. It's Jimmy. They have released him from prison. It appears you were correct, and he was not the killer. It was Betty or Lady Beatrice, whatever you want to call her."

"Wait, what? How did this all come about?"

"It appears Betty journaled about everything, including framing Jimmy. And get this, she accidentally poisoned herself with eye drops, of all things. Made herself so sick that she passed out and fell down the stairs. Ironically, she died. When they investigated her death, they found the jour-nals."

"Holy cow! That's amazing! I am happy for Jimmy. And now the others can all rest in peace."

"Oh honey, that's the other thing. Timothy and Jessica are alive! They lied to draw the actual killer out. And Jessica is pregnant. She isn't out of the woods yet. She is stable in a medical coma until they can take the baby safely and get a bullet fragment out."

"What about Richard? Is he really dead, or is he alive?"

Danielle's heart pounded in her chest, and her mind swirled. There was no way he survived those wounds, but her heart hoped.

"No, baby. He is dead. I am sorry. I know how much you loved him. Please come home. We will help you through whatever you are going through."

The tears flowed freely down her cheeks. She couldn't go back. This was her home now. Going back would be too painful. Too many ghosts and memories.

"Mom, I'm not coming back. I started a new life here in a small town in Pennsylvania. I have a good job. A nice little place of my own. I have made new friends. Now that the killer is dead, I can tell you why I left. I am pregnant with Richard's baby. It wasn't safe for me to tell before. I hope you understand, Mom."

"Danielle, thank you for finally being honest with me. I understand, honey. Can we come to visit?"

"I would love for you to come to visit. Please tell Jimmy, I am happy for him. And send my love to Timothy and Jessica. I gotta get ready for work, Mom. I love you."

"I love you too."

Danielle got ready for her shift at work. Pete was picking her up because she had heard a noise coming from her car the day before. He had said he would bring her to work and bring her car into his shop. It was convenient that he was an auto repair mechanic. It wasn't long before he knocked on her door. When she opened it up, she found him standing with a bag of groceries.

"What is all this?"

"It's dinner for later. I figured I would cook you dinner tonight after I pick you up."

"Pete, you are already doing so much for me. I can't keep letting you do all this."

"Why not? I am not asking for anything in return. Not even a relationship. You are a hard-working woman in a tough spot. You shouldn't have to do all this alone."

"I do have family, Pete. Just because I haven't talked about them doesn't mean they don't care about me. I have kept them in the dark since I left. They didn't even know I was pregnant till this morning."

"Okay, so why did you run away if they are a loving family? I don't get it."

"It's really complicated, Pete. I will fill you in on our way to my work."

On the short ride to the diner, Danielle filled Pete in on why she left everyone and everything she had known in life to raise her child on her own. When he parked the car, he turned in his seat and stared at her with compassion in his eyes. He ran his hand through his hair and then scratched the scruff of his beard.

"So you are telling me your ex-fiancée was a member of some big wealthy family that became the target of a serial killer? Which turned out to be another member of the family nobody knew about?"

"Yup. Sounds crazy and something completely out of some movie plot, but that was my life for the last six months."

"No wonder you took off and wanted no one from your past to know where you were. But, I don't understand why you don't want to go back. You have a family to help you out."

"It's hard to explain. At first, I had no proper plan. I just knew I needed to leave and not go back. There was no doubt in my mind that I was in danger if anyone found out about my baby. Then I wound up here in this town, and it felt like home so quickly. Like I have always belonged. Now I have put roots down, and I don't want to leave. I want to raise my child here, not in East Hampton."

"I can understand all of that. Thank you for trusting me with your story and your past, Danielle. It means the world to me."

"It is the least I can do for you, Pete. You deserve to know my story with all the help you have been giving me."

She quickly gave him a peck on the cheek and exited the car. He watched her enter the diner and then drove to his shop to work on her car. The fact she came from money had been a shock. She didn't seem like the typical rich girl stereotype. He was glad he hadn't known beforehand. It helped him to get to know her better with no preconceived notions.

Danielle's shift flew by and when it was time for her to go home, Pete was patiently waiting for her outside. He was leaning on the hood of her car with a bouquet of wildflowers. She smiled as he opened the car door for her and helped her in while handing her the flowers. She appreciated the chivalry he had, but she also didn't want him to think she was some damsel in distress who needed a knight in shining armor to rescue her.

"Hey Pete, did you figure out what was wrong with my car?"

"Absolutely, it was the right front tie rod. It's all fixed now."

"Thanks. What do I owe you?"

"Nothing."

"Pete, you can't just fix my car for free. I have money to pay you. Your time and energy are worth something. Not to mention the parts."

"I want to fix your car for free. Let me take care of you, Danielle. Why can't you do that?"

"I don't need you to take care of me. There is no reason for you to. I am not some damsel in distress. I appreciate everything you have done, but I never want to feel I owe you anything or that I am taking advantage of your kindness. So please tell me what I owe you."

"Okay, Okay. I get it. Six hundred dollars is what you owe me for fixing your car."

There was a little grit to his voice like he was trying not to clench his teeth. She couldn't understand why he felt so compelled to do everything for her. The rest of the drive to her cottage was awkwardly silent. Pete's brows furrowed as he stared at the road ahead of them, and his hands were tightly gripping the steering wheel. This was a different side of him.

When they got to her cottage, Pete parked the car and exited it, leaving the keys dangling in the ignition. He said nothing and just walked to his pickup truck. Danielle sat in the passenger side of her car, watching him with confusion. She grabbed her keys and left the vehicle.

Standing in front of her cottage door, she turned and watched as he pulled out of the driveway. He looked her way out of his side window and stopped as she gestured with both her hands out, questioning what was happening. The window slid down.

"What?"

Danielle didn't know how to feel. She didn't want him treating her like a damsel in distress like she needed him, but she was realizing deep down she wanted him in her life.

"Your money is inside. I have to go get it for you. And I thought you were making me dinner tonight?"

"You can drop the money off to me at my shop tomorrow. As for dinner, you just told me you don't need me to do anything for you. You don't want to feel obligated to me, so I guess you are making your own dinner tonight. By the way, add thirty dollars to that bill for the groceries."

Her heart sank. She had hurt him without realizing what she had done. After all of his kindness, she had stuck a knife in his heart. The window went up and he drove away. As he did, the tears welled up in her eyes. She whispered to the night sky.

"I don't need you, but I do want you in my life."

She couldn't believe she had messed things up so badly with Pete. Whether she wanted a romantic relationship with him, she honestly didn't know, but he had been a good friend since day one. How was she going to fix this?

The first thing the next morning, Danielle headed over to Pete's garage. She had to apologize, and she had to figure out how to fix their friendship. When she pulled up, the garage door was open, and she saw Pete standing next to a convertible and a tall, curvy blonde. The blonde was animated as she spoke with Pete, presumably trying to explain what was wrong with her car. Occasionally, she flipped her hair with her hand and tilted her head. She was flirting with him, and it surprised Danielle to find out that didn't sit well with her.

She never considered herself a jealous person. This feeling that was bubbling inside her wasn't quite a rage, but it was unsettling nevertheless. As she got out of her car and closed the door behind her, she startled herself when the car door slammed shut. Pete and the blonde both looked in her direction.

The blonde ignored Danielle and went on with her flirtatious behavior while Pete took off his ball cap and wiped his forehead nervously. Danielle leaned back against her car, crossed her legs and her arms, and waited.

When the blonde's ride showed up for her and she left, Danielle watched as Pete took a deep breath and started walking over to her.

"Good morning, Danielle. Look, I owe you an apology."

"No, Pete. You don't. I owe you an apology. You have been nothing but kind and compassionate to me this entire time. I hurt you with my words last night and that was wrong."

"Okay. I accept your apology, but I still owe you an apology. I should not have just shut down and left last night. You aren't the only one with a past that haunts them."

Pete shoved his hands in his pockets and rocked back and forth on his heels. Danielle was even more confused than before.

"Okay, so tell me, Pete. You don't have to carry your past alone. Share the burden with me. That is what friends do."

"It is a long story. Have you eaten breakfast yet?"

"I have all day. It's my day off. No, I couldn't eat this morning."

"Let's go up to my apartment and I will cook us some breakfast while I tell you everything."

"Okay."

After Pete closed the garage door, he led Danielle up the stairs to his apartment above his shop. It was small, but surprisingly clean for a bachelor pad. She had a seat at the small kitchen table as he set to work making them breakfast.

"I wasn't always a nice guy. Actually, I was quite the opposite. I was an egotistical ass."

"That is really hard for me to believe."

"It's true. I was the hometown hero, the captain of the football team. My girlfriend was the captain of the cheer team."

"No way!"

"Yup, I thought I was god's gift to this entire town and made sure everyone knew it too."

"Pete, I can't see it. What made you change so drastically?"

Pete dashed into his bedroom and came out with a high school yearbook. Danielle flipped through it. There he was in all his glory on pretty much every page of the candids.

"I didn't care about the prom, honestly I didn't even want to go. The party was all I cared about. My girlfriend, though, wanted to be prom king and queen. It had been her childhood dream. I didn't understand. She had spent a lot of money on her dress and hair. She bought the tickets. The pictures she paid for. I rented a used tuxedo."

"Okay, so you made your girlfriend pay for prom. That doesn't mean you were a jerk."

"Well, we were there less than a half hour and I wanted to leave. Before the king and queen were announced. She begrudgingly left with me. We fought on the way to the party. At one point, she yelled at me to let her out of the car. I obliged. She started walking back to the prom. I watched in the rearview mirror as a car came speeding around the corner and hit her."

"Oh my god, Pete. That's awful. It still wasn't your fault, though."

"But it was. I was too concerned with what I wanted, what I felt I needed, that I didn't care about her happiness. If we had stayed at prom, she would have lived. If I had put her first, she would still be here."

Pete sat across from Danielle and put his head down on his arms. He sobbed.

"I get it now. You put everything you have into helping others because you feel your selfishness killed your girlfriend. You need to know, though, that you didn't kill her. She could have stayed in the car and just gone to the party. She was a little selfish, too. But you were both young, just kids. Don't punish yourself forever."

Lifting his head and wiping his tears, he looked at Danielle.

"I never looked at it like that."

"There needs to be balance and understanding in every relationship. Give and take. Too much, either way, is unhealthy."

"Now I understand what you were trying to say yesterday about not needing my help with every-thing."

"Yeah, about that. I may not need you to do everything, but that doesn't mean I don't want you in my life."

Pete smiled and tilted his head.

"What I am hearing is you want me?"

He wiggled his eyebrows and made Danielle laugh.

"Honestly, I don't know what I want. All I know is I was sad thinking you were out of my life. Just as sad as missing Richard. And when I saw that blonde flirting with you this morning, I felt something I have never felt before."

"Really? What did you feel?"

"Jealous."

"I kind of got that impression when you slammed your car door."

Danielle laughed.

"Would you believe me if I told you that was an accident?"

Pete stood up and took Danielle by the hand. He guided her out of her chair and into his arms, then kissed her gently on the lips.

"No more than you would believe me if I said kissing you just now was an accident."

Danielle leaned her head onto Pete's chest and just hugged him.

"I don't know if I am ready for all this yet. But I am willing to see where it goes."

279

CHAPTER TWENTY-SEVEN

Goodbye Betty

JIMMY HAD CONTACTED ARTHUR about Betty's remains and journals. They agreed to have a small private burial in the family cemetery. It was just the two of them as they placed the journals inside the casket with her. They felt it was important that no one would know where the journals were. They were sure they would safely bury the journals along with Betty. When they were finished and closed the casket, they let the workers know it was time to bury her.

They had no big send-off. No flowers. There were no mourners. Nobody was going to miss Betty. Her death hadn't really made big headlines other than it led to the revelation she had been a serial killer. Most people in the Hamptons had gone about their daily lives. It was just more fodder for the gossip mill until the next affair occurred or the next movie star bought a piece of property in the area.

There was only one person who even seemed to notice her obituary. Mike sat on his back deck overlooking the Atlantic ocean swirling his glass of whiskey as he read the small blurb about Betty and her death. Such a shame. Their one night together had left an impression on him. One he would not soon forget.

He watched the new nanny his wife had hired interacting with their kids on the beach. This time, his wife had gone out of her way to find the most unattractive woman she could find. He would have to find some other way to fulfill his needs. He scanned the beach for any beach bunnies, but had no luck. Betty would be hard to forget. He swigged the whiskey and poured himself another glass.

When Timothy was told that Betty had been buried. He felt the weight of the world lifted off his shoulders. She was gone for good. Now all that needed to happen was for Jessica to heal and their baby to be born safely.

Stella watched from a distance Betty's coffin being lowered into the ground. She took a deep breath and let it out slowly. She was glad to have closure on the entire ordeal, finally.

Arthur left the island to head home. He had contemplated telling Jimmy earlier about his plans to retire. However, he felt it wasn't the time or place. In the next coming days, he would set up meetings with a new attorney who he felt could help represent the family in the future. He felt the younger Gardiners needed a clean slate with someone new.

The new ferry had finally arrived, and Captain Bill was grumpily adjusting to running it. Things seemed to be slowly getting back to normal. The security crew was busy catching teenagers trespassing on the beaches and running off the tabloid reporters itching for their latest scoop.

Jimmy and Melissa spent the rest of the day riding the ATVs around the island. Just spending quality time with each other that didn't include investigating a serial killer. When they stopped on the southern beach, Jimmy pulled out a picnic blanket and basket. Melissa smiled as she watched him set everything up.

After he completed the setup, he grabbed her hand and walked her over to the blanket. Then he got down on one knee and produced a ring from his pocket.

"I figured I better ask you properly and make it official. Melissa, will you marry me?"

"Yes, Jimmy. Absolutely, yes!"

He stood up and picked her up in his arms and swung her around.

"I feel like the luckiest man alive right now."

"Well, I feel like the luckiest woman."

Her lips brushed against his, and their bodies melted together onto the blanket. After several hours, they lay entwined in each other's arms, wrapped in the blanket, listening to the waves crash against the shore. Jimmy wanted to stay like that forever, but he was afraid Melissa would get cold.

"I guess we better head back up to the Manor house."

"Why Jimmy? I am content to stay here in your arms for eternity, or at least for tonight."

"Aren't you afraid you will get cold?"

"Not when I have you to keep me warm."

"And what if I get cold?"

"Hmm, I guess I will just have to heat you up."

Jimmy kissed her passionately. They spent the night under the stars, knowing they had the rest of their lives together.

Chapter Twenty-Eight

New Beginnings

IT WAS MID-JULY WHEN the team of doctors assembled to perform the cesarean section on Jessica and to remove the bullet fragment. They felt the baby was developed enough to survive outside her womb. The longer they kept her in the medically induced coma, the more she was at risk for long-term damage. After several discussions, they decided with Timothy to perform the surgery.

Timothy paced back and forth in the waiting room. Allison, Jack, Jimmy, and Melissa were all there with him. A doctor came out and Timothy stopped pacing.

"I am here to give you an update. The baby is out. They have brought her to the NICU. You will be able to visit her shortly. As for your wife, the surgery to remove the bullet fragment is under-way. So far, everything looks good. We will let you know when the surgery is complete, and they move her into recovery."

"Thanks, Doc. It's a girl, that's awesome!"

Everyone gathered around Timothy and started congratulating him.

***

Back in Pennsylvania, Danielle was working when she had contractions. At first, she thought they were just Braxton Hicks, but then they got more intense and started coming more regularly. When her water broke, Wendy called an ambu-lance, and then she called Pete.

Danielle had never experienced such intense pain. As she rode in the ambulance, fear crept into her mind. She was only just seven months pregnant. Would the baby be big enough and developed to survive outside the protection of her womb? The Paramedics did their best to keep her calm. They arrived at the hospital in no time and they wheeled her quickly into a labor and delivery room. Pete arrived just in time to help her through the pushing. He held her hand as she squeezed it with each contraction. A few pushes and the baby was born.

"It's a boy. Congratulations Mom and Dad. Since he is premature, we need to bring him over to the NICU."

The nurses showed Danielle her baby right before they whisked him away into the NICU.

"He's beautiful."

"Just like his Momma."

Pete kissed Danielle's forehead.

"I think we should name him Pete. Pete Gardiner. After the two men I have ever loved and who have loved me unconditionally."

"Danielle, are you sure?"

"Absolutely!"

"Well, I guess if you are going to name your son after me, I better do the proper thing. Danielle, will you marry me?"

"Yes, Pete. I will marry you. Not because it's the proper thing to do, but because I love you with all my heart."

"I love you too, Danielle. I have since the first day I met you."

"I know. Thank you for being patient with me."

***

A few hours later, the doctors came back out to Timothy to give him an update on Jessica.

"Timothy, we have great news. The surgery was a success. Your wife is in recovery. As soon as she is fully awake, you can visit with her. She still has a lot of physical therapy and occupational therapy to go through for a full recovery, but she is strong and young. We have faith that she will be fine. She may have difficulty with speech too at first, so give her time."

"Thank you, Doc. I appreciate everything you have done for our family."

"Go see your daughter and I will have the nurses come to get you when your wife is awake in recovery."

Timothy hugged Allison, Jack, Jimmy, and Melissa goodbye and thanked them for sitting with him, and then he went to meet his daughter.

***

A year flew by, and Timothy shuffled through the mail he had just come back from retrieving. He smiled as he saw the return address of the first letter. It was from Jimmy and Melissa. By the look and feel of the envelope, he assumed it was their wedding invitation. The second took him by surprise. The return address was from Pennsylvania and it was from Danielle. He brought the letters out to the patio, where Jessica was sipping her morning tea.

"Looks like we have mail from the States. I think one is Jimmy and Melissa's wedding invite. The other is from Danielle."

They had moved to their cottage in Ireland as soon as Jessica had recovered enough and baby Samantha could travel. She opened the one from Jimmy first. It indeed was the wedding invitation. The date was in September. She was relieved to see they were not holding the wedding on the island. Jimmy and Melissa were very respectful of Timothy and Jessica and their powerful feelings about never setting foot on the island again.

Then Jessica opened the letter from Danielle. It was an invitation to her wedding the weekend after Jimmy's. She hadn't heard from Danielle other than some get-well cards and flowers sent to the hospital since her own wedding. She understood the distance that had formed between them with everything they both had gone through. Jessica was happy for Danielle, and it thrilled her to be invited to witness her new beginning.

"Well, it looks like we need to plan a trip to the States in September! We have two weddings to attend!"

"That's great! It will be nice to see everyone again. Samantha can get to know her extended family. I will go start making travel plans."

* * *

Jimmy and Melissa spent the year planning their wedding. They had just sent out all the invitations when things got busy on the island. Jimmy wasn't too concerned about the uptick in trespassers. However, it was unsettling after the relatively quiet year they had when they found a few of the graves at the family cemetery disturbed. Although he chalked it up to teenagers looking for pirate treasure. Nothing further transpired afterward, which validated his belief.

***

Danielle and Pete bought a house together and planned their own wedding. Danielle's family visited her frequently. However, she still refused to go back to visit her hometown. The ghosts of her past were just too much for her to face. They were looking forward to their nuptials within the next few months.

***

Allison remained the CEO of Cromwell Real Estate Corporation, yet she did most of her work from the home office Jessica and Timothy had built for her at the cottage. She had moved with them to help Timothy care for Samantha and Jessica.

***

Jack moved into Jessica's home in Preston and opened up his own restaurant.

***

Arthur had retired, leaving his colleague, Mr. Whitty, in charge of helping the Gardiner family with their legal issues and helping them run their business.

***

Life had become all that they had envisioned, happy and free of a serial killer stalking them or their loved ones. Jessica finally knew who she was. She was a wife and mother.

CHAPTER TWENTY-NINE

The End

The End…. or is it just the
Beginning?

Acknowledgements

A big thank you to my family and friends who have supported this journey of mine into authorship. There are way too many of you to single out individually! I appreciate you all!

Thank you to my ARC team who have been a tremendous help in catching any missed mistakes that occur throughout the writing and editing process.

R.K., Mr. Kaplan would be proud!

L.C., thank you for utilizing your editing expertise!

K.S., B.T., A.S., M.M., thank you for being on my team. Also, thank you for taking the time to write honest reviews and recommend my books! You all rock!

Thank you to all the administrators of the numerous Facebook groups that allow Independent authors to promote their books. You are all amazing! You help us to get our books noticed!

Thank you M.B., my badass corrections nurse friend who provided me with much insight into prison life.

About Author

A paraeducator, novice genealogist, turned author D.M. Foley is an award-winning writer. Her first book, The Lyons Garden Book One Family Ties, received The New York Best Sellers Gold Award in December 2021. She lives in Southeastern, Ct, with her husband, three sons, and her mom.

You can follow her on her social media accounts at:

D.M. Foley - Author Page on Facebook

@d.m._foley on Instagram and TikTok

@DMFoleyauthor on Twitter

If you want exclusive content please go to her website and sign up for her newsletter.

https://dm-foley-author-p7wdjh.mailer-page.io/

Contact Information:

d.m.foleyauthor@gmail.com

D.M. Foley

P.O. Box 735

54 Main Street

Jewett City, CT

06351

Books In This Trilogy

Family Ties The Lyons Garden Book One
Erasing Secrets The Lyons Garden Book Two
Pawns The Lyons Garden Book Three